WHAT IF WE DO

SUSAN RENEE

Editing by Brandi Zelenka, Notes in the Margin
Reader Team: Kristan Anderson, Stephani Brown, Jenn Hager, Jennifer Wilson
Formatted by Doug Huston
Cover Design by Quirky Bird Covers

Chapter 1

Scarlett

One Week Ago

"SON OF A MOTHERFUCKING LIMP DICK TAINT STAIN!" I slam my ornately decorated fall bouquet to the ground, gold-glittered spirals gliding across the floor as flower petals and stems break apart on contact. "I should have known!"

An entire sanctuary full of people turn at my outburst, which pisses me off even more now that I've made myself a spectacle.

Go big or go home, right?

"FUCK!"

"Shhh, Scarlett," Maria, my Maid of Honor sputters, closing the narthex doors and trying to avoid a scene. "Maybe he's just…you know, stuck in the bathroom."

"HE'S AFRAID TO SHIT IN PUBLIC, MARIA! YOU KNOW THIS!" I shout. "He wouldn't be caught dead shitting in a church." A low rumble of laughter comes from the other side of the door as I pace back and forth in the narthex where I had been patiently waiting with my bridesmaids to make our grand entrance. I was supposed to marry the love of my life today, but apparently, my asshat of a fiancé had other plans.

"Okay so maybe he just needs a little more time. Maybe his shoelace broke. Or his pants ripped."

I cock my head at my other bridesmaid, Jess. "Do you know how many hours I put into planning this…this…" I flail my arms. "Party? Do you know how many sleepless nights I had trying to plan this wedding so everything would be perfect for him? I wanted a fun Halloween themed wedding but noooooo. Mark said that would be classless for his line of work so I gave in and planned this fucking beautiful day."

"I know, babe."

"And I look amazing!" My chin begins to quiver. "And I feel…I felt…"

Aaaaand cue the waterworks. "I felt beautiful today."

Jess pulls me in for a hug. "Scarlett, honey, you do look amazing. Nothing about what's happening changes that."

"I fell in love with this dress and now it's…tainted. Everybody came here today for this grand event that Mark paid for! Why would he do this if he had no intention of showing up?"

"Could he have been in a car accident?" Maria asks with a cringe.

Feeling terribly guilty for my outburst when it is entirely possible that Mark was in an accident on the way here, I start to panic.

"Oh God! What if you're right? My phone. Who has my phone? I need my phone!"

"Here, I have it!" Jess dips into her pocket and pulls out my cellphone. I tap it on and open my LIFE360 app to see where he's located and my face falls.

"He's at the fucking office."

It doesn't take a genius to figure out what this means.

He chose work over our wedding day.

He chose work over me.

He doesn't want to marry me.

Ripping my veil from my elegantly twisted and pinned hair, I drop to the floor. "It's over."

"Oh Scarlett." Maria and Jess both try their best to comfort me but sometimes a girl just needs to cry it out before she can pull up her big girl pants and figure out a way to make the sweetest lemonade out of the big fat lemons she's been tossed.

"What am I going to do?" I ask them, my fears and self-pity finally surfacing.

Maria takes my hand, giving it a supportive squeeze. "You're going to do just what you're doing because your feelings are valid. Be sad. Be furious. Be whatever you want to be."

"Yeah." Jess nods. "And then we're going to go drink all the top shelf alcohol at the country club because Mark is footing the bill. He may think he's a good businessman but he has yet to experience the hell that is a woman scorned on her wedding day."

I snort. "An angry and petty as fuck woman scorned on her wedding day."

"Amen to that, Sis!" My bridesmaids give each other a high five. "We'll be right by your side all night."

———

Okay, small confession here. I think deep down I've always known Mark Adelman was not the love of my life. I mean, did I love him? Yes. But if I'm being honest with myself as I reflect on what happened last weekend, I know he didn't really believe in me.

In who I am.

In who I want to be.

He didn't see my work as viable or as a benefit to the community. I've always had this feeling, though he never said the words outright, that he thinks being a social media influencer isn't a real job and that it's all fun and games telling followers about my favorite shoes or my favorite books or my favorite new kitchen tool. He has no idea just how daunting it can be. The hours of research, website building, content planning for social media, the constant array of messages from one company or another wanting you to be a part of their brand. It's much harder work than anyone gives it credit for, but I ignored his little snide comments over the years. I even ignored his silence when trying to tell him about some of the best parts of my job. The money. The unique gifts. The extra perks. The friends I've made along the way. He didn't care. I chose to keep my chin up anyway and continue doing what made me happy…even if the feeling of inadequacy stirred in my soul more often than I care to admit.

"Have you spoken to him?"

"He texted me the day after. Two words. Can you guess what they were?"

"I'm working?" Maria guesses.

I shake my head. "Guess again."

Jess narrows her eyes, tapping her fingernails on the tabletop. "I'm sorry?"

"Not even that," I scoff. "His text just said I can't."

Maria's brow peaks. "I can't? Seriously?"

I nod silently as Mark's words sink in.

"Fucking Asshole," Jess murmurs.

"Yep."

"So, what are you going to do about the honeymoon?" Maria takes a sip of her coffee. "You guys are supposed to be on a plane in a few days for New Orleans."

I roll my eyes. "He never wanted to go to New Orleans. He wanted to go to Fiji or someplace remote and tropical. You know, where all the rich people go."

"Didn't he agree to New Orleans for you?"

I nod. "Yeah. He secured VIP tickets for us to attend the famous Once Upon a Halloween Night party together. It's at Generations Hall in the French Quarter and it's one of the biggest Halloween parties of the year. I've been dying to go since I was in high school. So, he agreed to a few days in New Orleans if I agreed to a private Caribbean cruise on his friend's yacht after that. That's why we decided to wait a week between our wedding and our honeymoon. Now that's all fucked.

Jess shakes her head. "No girl. You've got that all wrong."

"What do you mean?"

"You're going on that honeymoon."

"What?"

"Yeah." She nods with a smirk on her face like she just planned the best prank of her life. "You're totally going and you're taking every single one of your followers with you. And it's all on Mark's dime."

I shake my head. "Sorry. No. I have no interest in putting myself on the yacht that belongs to one of Mark's friends or…sleezy businesspeople. No thank you."

"Not the cruise," she says. "Fuck the cruise. Let him eat that trip and explain it to his friend if he hasn't already. I'm talking about the Halloween party."

Hmm. I'm intrigued.

"I'm listening…."

"You already have the tickets, don't you?"

"Yeah."

She sits back in her chair with a smile and gestures to my phone. "Then get on that thing and invite someone to go with you and take that fucking trip. Go. Have a fucking blast without the man who is footing the bill. Do all the things. You can consider it revenge if you want to, but really, you deserve to get away and do something that makes your soul happy."

The idea of attending the Halloween party without Mark does excite me to some level, but "Who would I ask to be my plus one?"

Maria shrugs. "Anybody. Put it on your platforms. See if you get a bite. My guess is someone out there wouldn't mind a free trip to New Orleans and to one of the biggest Halloween parties of the year."

"You mean you guys don't want to go?"

Jess shakes her head. "Babe, you're a social media influencer and your followers love you! Take them on this trip and show all those jilted lovers out there that this is how you stand up and take what you deserve. Scarlett Dayne doesn't just lay down and take it up the ass. She deserves the foreplay. The fun. The excitement. The adventure. You can do this."

A smile broadens across my face. "You know, I think you might be right."

"Hell, yes, I'm right." She gives me a high five. "Now let's work on what you're going to say and how you're going to choose and then we'll create the perfect video for you to put out there."

I swallow down my mimosa, because what's better to drink when you've been drinking for days and you're hung over than more alcohol and sit up in my chair. "Let's get to work."

Chapter 2

Oliver

When the siren goes off the team hits the ice in celebration of our win. A hard-fought game for sure, but we had no injuries tonight and that surely paid off with a victory against Phoenix.

"This game goes to Bear!" I exclaim when we enter the locker room. I give our burly goalie a fist bump and a bro hug as the team cheers him on. "Expertly maneuvered game tonight, man. You were on fire tonight."

"Yeah, my knees will be telling me that through the next four ice baths, but I wouldn't have it any other fucking way. We do what we gotta do to take what's ours."

Barrett "The Bear" Cunningham joined the team last year from Toronto as our starting goalie after our goalie of six years was traded. We weren't sure how things were going to go with him given his new status on the team, but he's shown us every step of the way that he deserves the job and he excels at it. It's been an absolute pleasure having him on the team.

"You deserve a beer after tonight, Bear!" Griffin caps his shoulder. "First one's on me."

"I may be a little late," he tells us. "Ice bath first, then stretches before I shower and get out of here."

"No problem, man." I tell him with a nod. "Take your time. We'll see you at Jay's?"

He nods. "I'll be there."

—

Since we don't board the plane for New Orleans until eleven tomorrow, we all celebrate with a beer and the juiciest fucking burger Jay's Sports Bar can whip up and they do not disappoint.

"What the fuck is she doing now?" Ledger says, shaking his head at his phone. The baffled smirk on his face tells me he's not as pissed as he sounds.

"She who?" I swallow my bite. "You're not still creeping all over Marlee's social media are you?" Marlee Remington works in the front office and has for a couple of years now. She's the Events and Operations Manager, which means every event that includes a member of the team goes through her. She knows where every one of us is supposed to be, when we're supposed to be there and what we're supposed to be doing. We see her daily if not every couple of days and it's no secret Ledger has eyes for her. "Honestly why don't you just ask her out already?"

Ignoring my question completely, he shakes his head and answers, "No. Not Marlee. My cousin."

"Who's your cousin? She famous?"

"Depends on who you ask, I guess. Her name is Scarlett Dayne. She's an influencer so I guess to a large enough group of people out there, she's famous, yeah. She's the one I mentioned last week. The one with the wedding."

I snap my fingers after recalling his story. "Oh yeah, the one who got left at the altar?"

"Yep. That's the one."

Cringing, I lift my beer and take another gulp. "That must've been a terrible day for her."

"Well, if you go by the outburst we all heard from the back of the church when she realized her fiancé didn't show up, then yeah. You would feel terrible for her."

"Uh oh." I smile. "Sounds like a but coming on."

"Buuut. She spent the rest of the night partying like it was her twenty-first birthday totally on the fiancé's dime so…" Ledger shrugs with a laugh. "I guess things didn't turn out so badly. I don't know."

"So, what's she doing now? Throwing all this guy's shit into the ocean? Pawning it off? Starring in a new reality tv show? The Un-housewives of L.A.?"

"No." He huffs a laugh again. "She's going on her honeymoon."

My brows lift in pure morbid curiosity. "With the guy who left her?"

Ledger shakes his head. "No. She's going on her own but she just put out a video asking for someone to go with her as her plus one to that big Once Upon a Halloween Night event in New Orleans. That's why they chose New Orleans for their honeymoon destination. If I remember correctly, my mom mentioned they were taking the guy's yacht out on a cruise after the party but Scarlett really wanted to attend this Halloween shindig."

"I've heard that's the party of the year. What influencer wouldn't want to be there? She sounds like a smart woman."

"You want to go with her?" He glances my way from his phone. "I'll put in a good word for you."

"What? No." I frown. "Why would I want to do that?"

"I don't know." He shrugs and pauses as if he's thinking about it. "I mean, she's a great girl, as far as dates go. Fun, talkative. Conversational. She was always a spunk of personality growing up and in our adult years she's a been a fan of the team, but she's not a fan girl…if you know what I mean."

"You mean she's not going to toss her tits in my direction and beg me to motorboat her in the hotel hallway?" I scoff teasingly. "No fucking thank you."

"Exactly." He laughs but then I watch as his smile fades. His eyes still on her video. "Actually, my mom said she was devastated last week once the circus ended. She's a good person. Hardworking. Compassionate. She may have been engaged to a filthy rich fiancé but she's far from a trophy wife. She's not like that at all. She didn't deserve to be treated the way she was by this guy. He's a glorified douche with a capital D. Scarlett wants to earn her spot in the world, you know? Like us."

I cock my head. "Have we really earned our place in the world? Playing hockey, I mean?"

"Fuck man," he huffs a laugh. "If we weren't earning our place on the team, our fans and everyone else paying our salaries would drop us like a sack of hot shit."

"I suppose that's true." Gesturing toward his phone with my chin, I ask to see a picture of her. When Ledger turns his phone around and I see her in the video she's made, I must admit, she's not at all how I had imagined.

I don't know why I was expecting some blonde haired, blue-eyed valley girl, but Scarlett Dayne is anything but. Dark, burgundy-colored waves blow in the breeze around her heart-shaped face. Her mossy green eyes sparkle with excitement as she tells her story to all her fans. But what makes something in me sit up and take notice of her are the freckles peppered across her cheeks and the way her nose scrunches a little when she smiles.

She's cute.

No. She's more than cute.

She's pretty.

Beautiful even.

"I mean, you're going to be in town anyway," Ledger murmurs next to me, noticing my piqued interest.

"Just for the game though and then we fly home."

"Yeah, but we have two days off before we fly to Chicago. You can stay back and then meet us there. No problem."

I glance up at the televisions hanging on the wall in the front of the bar. Two football games and another hockey game play on the screens. The hockey game looks to be the Red Tails and the Bay Scrapers. Red Tails are up two to one. My brother-in-law, Milo Landric is looking pretty sharp. I wouldn't mind sitting at home and watching the end of this game.

"Why do you want me to do this so badly?"

My best friend gives me half a shrug and leans back against the booth. "Because the more I think about it, the more I think the two of you might get along really well."

"How's that?"

"Come on, Oli. You're a fun guy and you're single and she's…" He shakes his head trying to find the right words. "She's looking to be a little adventurous while she finds her footing after all the hurt she's been through. Plus, if you do this, I won't have to worry that she's being taken advantage of. She'll be safe with you. New Orleans isn't necessarily the place to mess with strangers, you know?"

"And L.A. is?"

"You know what I mean."

My elbows on the table, I press my forehead to my palm. "Why do I feel like this is one of those rom com stories my sister edits being written right in front of my face?"

"I mean never say never, I guess." He smirks and nudges my arm. "Hey maybe we'll be related through marriage someday."

"In your fucking dreams, Ledge."

His brows pinch together as he shakes his head. "No, not in my fucking dreams, dude. Those are saved for someone else." He leans over and lays his head against my shoulder. Before I can shrug him off he says, "But maybe my swooniest, fan-girliest, oh-my-gosh-I-hope-Oliver-and-I-get-to-be-cousins-one-day dreams."

"You know it's never going to happen, right?"

"Come on." He nudges a little harder. "Just look at this like a super fun blind date with a beautiful girl who just happens to be related to me so if on the off chance, you two were to one day fall in love and get married…"

This time I do push him off of me. "Yeah, yeah, yeah. I think 've heard enough."

"Soooo, is that a yes?"

Is it a yes?

Is this even remotely a good idea?

What if it ends up being a terrible mistake?

What's the worst that can happen?

She ends up crying the entire time forcing me to be the nice guy and perk her back up?

She doesn't show up and I catch the next flight home?

I suppose I could at the very least meet the girl and see what happens.

Not like I have anything else to do.

Besides, with Ledger, there's no way I'm getting out of this.

Unless she doesn't pick me.

Except if I'm going all in with this, she better fucking pick me.

I take a deep breath and roll my eyes but only because Ledger is in my face giving me the worst puppy dog eyes I've ever seen. He needs help.

"Okay. Fine. I'll do it."

"Fuck, yeah, you will!"

"IF…" I raise my pointer finger. "She picks me. It's perfectly fine if she wants to go with someone else."

"Whatever." Ledger smiles and starts moving his thumbs across his phone. "I'm DM-ing her right now to tell her you're in."

Once he's done, he tosses his phone to the side and picks up his burger, eating halfway through it in two bites. The rest of us chat about tonight's game, the goals scored by Griffin and August, and the amazing saves Bear had. Hours go by as they do when we're hanging at Jay's. The Redtails game ended an hour ago. They kicked ass as always which definitely hyped up the guys hanging out as we face off against them in the not too distant future. It's always fun getting to play some hockey with my brother-in-law and his friends.

Just as I'm thinking about leaving, my phone buzzes in my pocket.

Charlee: Hey brother! Good game tonight! The new guy is looking amazing!

Me: Hey! Thanks! I see you guys are winning as well. The bar is replaying the east coast games here. Looking forward to our future faceoff. *smirk emoji*

Charlee: Is it bad that I wish you could both win when that happens?

Me: Yes. You should only be cheering for flesh and blood.

Charlee: LOL. In your dreams bro. Hate to tell you but I think you're going down.

Me: HA! Is that what Milo tells you?

Charlee: I mean they're the champions to beat. They just took the cup last season.

Me: Nowhere to go but down, Sis.

Charlee: Oooh buuurn! Those are some fightin' words!

Me: Hey, I'm glad you texted. Looks like I'm staying in New Orleans an extra day for an event. So, I'll fly to Chicago before our matchup. Alright if I stay with you and Milo for the night before the game? I wouldn't mind hanging with my baby sis for a night if she'll have me."

Charlee: Milo says, "Oooh sleeping with the enemy. I like it."

Me: LOL perfect. Can't wait.

Charlee: See you then! Love you bro!

Me: Love you, Sis!

I'm about to return my phone to my pocket when I get another notification via social media.

Scarlett: Hi! My cousin, Ledger sent me a message about your interest in being my plus one for the Once Upon a Halloween Night event in New Orleans!

"Well, that was fast. She contacted me already."
"Who?" Ledger asks. "Scarlett?"
"Yeah."
"What did she say?"
"She wants to know if I'm really interested."

"Well tell her you're interested, Magallan!"

Me: Uh, hey. Yeah. I'm game if you are. I mean if there's someone else you would rather take, that's totally fine.

Scarlett: No. I think this is great! Ledger has said wonderful things about you in the past and now I won't have to worry about someone only wanting to hang out with me because I'm...well...mildly famous on the internet. *cringe emoji* Sorry if that sounded a little conceited.

Me: Not at all. I totally get it. Ledger constantly treats me like the hot sex symbol that I clearly am. I think he even used the word 'swoon' earlier. *wink emoji*

"Dude, you did not just say that," Ledger says, reading over my shoulder.

I chuckle. "Sure as fuck did."

Scarlett: OMG you're perfect! I like you already! *laugh emoji* Okay, so do you have a costume?

Me: Nope. Not yet. And honestly, I'm not sure how much time I'll have to get one. We fly to New Orleans tomorrow for a game so I'll already be in town. I'm sure there's somewhere down there where I can grab one.

Scarlett: Oh great! Yeah! There are several cool shops down here for that sort of thing. Especially given the city is hosting the largest Halloween party of the year. Any chance you can pick me up at the airport? Then we can find you a costume.

Me: Yeah, I can do that. Send me your flight info. I'll get a car and meet you there.

Scarlett: Perfect. Thank you so much for your willingness to attend this event with me Oliver! I really appreciate it! It's going to be a blast!

Me: Looking forward to it. Oh, should I come up with a meeting spot or something at the airport?

Scarlett: Oh. Ummmm *smirk emoji* I don't think that will be necessary.

Me: Okay...

Scarlett: Trust me. You'll know who I am. I promise.

Me: I trust you. *wink emoji* Have a great flight! I'll see you on Saturday.

I close out of my app and shove my phone back in my pocket.

"So, it's done?"

I nod to an excited Ledger. "It's done. Picking her up from the airport on Saturday."

He gives himself an appreciative nod. "Fuckin' right. I just set up my cousin with my best friend."

"For the record," I remind him, "This is the first and only time I'll allow it because it's not really a set up. It's more like…me doing you a favor."

"Yeah, yeah." He laughs. "Call it what you want. I'll just call it now. Y'all are gettin' hitched."

"Fuck you, dude."

Chapter 3

Oliver

Last night's game was a total shit show and I've been bitter about it since I left the arena. Not only did the Gators play a rough game, but I also played like shit and that's not like me. My mind wandered a little too much and my focus got away from the puck. My teammates have every right to be pissed at me, but some of them didn't play very well either. Harrison had five or six turnovers throughout the night, August was checked into the wall and got a bloody nose when a fight ensued, and Bear let three pucks into the net.

Like I said, shit show.

But it's over now and the best thing we can do is let the loss roll off our backs and move forward, vowing to never let those same mistakes happen again. The team left last night to fly back home before our games in Chicago, so that leaves me here to have a fun couple of days off. Once I figure out where I need to park at the airport, I head inside to wait for Scarlett to arrive.

"Eleven-seventeen. Sunshine Airlines Gate B." I read the message on my Apple watch one more time so I'm sure to get it right. I texted Scarlett earlier today to let her know what I'm wearing, black pants and a green Henley top, so she can find me. I'm able to watch the plane pull in so I know she made it, but what I'm not ready for is the sight before my eyes a little over ten minutes later when she's walking toward me down the terminal. Her satiny red hair in ringlets clipped behind her head, she has the face of an angel. She doesn't wear a ton of makeup, which I like. It leaves room for those freckles I noticed before, which look even cuter in real life, and her goofy grin as she practically skips to me makes me beam right back at the beautiful stranger.

"You must be Oliver."

"And you must be Scarlett."

"What gave me away?" She twirls in front of me and I'm not sure if I should laugh or tell her how goddamn sexy she looks right now.

"That's uh…quite the airplane wardrobe you chose, huh?"

"Do you like it?"

"Of course. I mean, you look…" My eyes dart up and down her curvy body as she stands before me in a rather expensive-looking wedding dress made up of tiers of gathered ruffles on the bottom and a sleeveless deep V-neck adorned with sparkling beads and pearls on top. "Pardon me for saying, but you look sexy as hell in this dress."

Her eyes light up at my compliment. "You really think so?"

I nearly scoff because fuck, I have to focus on not drooling just looking at her. Swiping my hand down my face, I linger at my chin as I nod. "Uh, yeah. I do. This was to be your wedding dress?"

"Yep," she says with a pop to the P. "And now it's nothing but trash."

My brows peak. "What?"

"Yeah. The dress is shit to me now. It was the most beautiful thing I had ever seen and when I put it on, I felt like I was legit royalty," she sighs in a huff and then shrugs. "But now. Fuck it. His money paid for it and I'll never get to wear it ever again, so I'm wearing it today and we're going to trash it together."

"What? Trash it? Are you insane?"

There's no way that dress didn't cost a fortune.

She laughs. "Nope. Not insane. Just ready to have an absolute blast today and if this thing turns into rags because of all the fun we're having, so be it. And then I'll be able to say good riddance to bad fucking rubbish. You still in Magallan?"

She pops her hip and waits for my reply, which comes just as naturally as taking her hand in mine. "Hell yeah, I'm in." I squeeze her hand for good measure. "Let's get your luggage and go have some fun."

"Great. I'm starving and ready for some southern barbecue."

"I know just the place."

———

"Mmmm! Oh, my God, this is delish! You weren't lying when you said you knew just the place, huh?"

I lick the sauce from my fingers. "Yeah. Bubba's is one of my favorite places to eat here. I tell everyone I know to come here when they're in town."

She smiles. "Sincere word of mouth from a celebrity. That's impressive."

"I don't know that I would consider myself a celebrity."

"Uh, I beg to differ," she scoffs with a hint of humor. "You make millions playing hockey for one of the best teams in the league."

"You wouldn't have thought that yesterday. Fuck, that game was brutal."

"I saw parts of it." She lifts her shoulder. "When one team wins, that means one team has to lose, right?"

"Yeah, I guess so."

"You'll get 'em next time. I have no doubt."

I wipe my mouth with my napkin and sit back in my chair. "So, tell me about you."

"You mean Ledger didn't give you my life story?" Her grin makes me smile and sends a bit of a jolt through my stomach at the same time. She seems so down to earth and easy going, which I very much appreciate.

"Nope. All he told me was that you're an influencer who had an unbelievably dreadful day. He told me why you're here and that you were looking for a plus one. Not to bring up a sour subject but I'm sorry about the wedding. No matter the circumstances, you didn't deserve to be disrespected like that."

She tries to shake it off like it's no big deal but I have a feeling deep down she's more bothered than she's letting on. "You know, sometimes life has a way of pointing you in a different direction. One completely opposite from where you thought you were going and you just have to learn to…be okay with it, I guess." She takes a sip of her beer before digging into another chicken wing. "He would've hated this, by the way."

"Bubba's?" I ask with a lift of my brows.

"Mhmm. He would've seen this as some trashy dive totally beneath him." She rolls her eyes and shakes her head. "I should've been more honest with myself. The stuffy Stepford wife life isn't me and even though it hurt at the time—I mean, he didn't even fucking show up—I know it's all for the best. I don't hate him." A small smirk plays across her lips. "But I'll definitely take advantage of his money since he already paid for this honeymoon."

"Savage," I tell her.

"Ha! That's me. Savage Scarlett."

"I dig it. So, what makes you happy? What sets your soul on fire?"

Her earthy green eyes meet mine and I swear to God they sparkle. "Living life to the fullest sets my soul on fire."

I cock my head to the side. "What do you mean by that?"

She leans forward, her gaze still holding mine. "I mean, do you ever have those moments where you're lying in bed thinking to yourself, 'I don't want to spend day after day in the same fucking cubicle or working for the same rich CEO who doesn't give two shits about your life.' I mean probably not in your case, since you play hockey and it's a sport I'm guessing you love it more than anything, but still. You get what I'm saying."

"Even playing a sport I love every day I totally get what you're saying, yeah."

She pulls her arms into her chest and takes a deep breath. "I just want to…live in the moment, you know? My job, although stressful at times, allows me experiences I would never have otherwise and I live for that. I look at every day as a gift. An opportunity to share something about life or the world around me with my followers and that's what makes me happy. Making people happy makes me happy."

"I think that's great. You certainly have the personality for what you do."

She beams. "Thank you. I appreciate that. I work hard, but I like to play harder. So, with that being said, we need to get you a killer costume for tonight." She bites into her chicken wing again, leaving sauce in the corner of her mouth and of course, on her fingers. Before I can even point it out to her though, she swipes a finger over the sauce on her lips and then wipes her hands on her dress, much to my shock and amusement.

"I could've gotten you more napkins, you know."

"What good are napkins when you have a perfectly good twenty-thousand-dollar dress to trash?" She laughs and then stands. "Come on, let's get out of here."

Chapter 4

Scarlett

"Okay, let's see what these look like before we look at anymore. If we're lucky, one of these will be the perfect costume for you." I pat the pile of costumes Oliver is carrying, internally taking note of how patient and easy going he's been while we've sifted through just about every adult costume in this boutique. "Dressing rooms are in the back."

"Alright." He turns toward the back of the store but then stops and looks back at me.

"What?"

"Well, come on! You have to be back here so I can put on a fashion show."

A huge smile spreads across my face and I clap my hands excitedly. "Eeeek! I was hoping you would say that! I'm so in!" Following Oliver to the back of the store, I take a seat in one of the chairs placed outside the dressing room so I can wait for his first reveal.

He comes out after a few minutes with his arms out, turning in a circle with a smirk on his face. "What do you think?"

Narrowing my eyes a bit, I shake my head. "I don't think I'm feeling the bell bottoms and groovy glasses. It's not...you."

"Good. I hate it." He laughs. "I just didn't want to upset you."

I giggle at his response. "Hey at least we're on the same page. And I'm pretty hard to offend so don't think you have to tiptoe around me. Fairly sure I've already lived through the most offensive experience of my life anyway."

His smile falls and he lowers his voice when he asks, "I know I haven't really mentioned it a lot but do you want to talk about it? I'm more than willing to listen if you want to vent, or, you know, cry or scream or whatever."

He's so sweet for offering. "That's very sweet of you, but no. I'm good," I say with a quick shrug and a bob to my head. "I mean it comes and goes, you know? Mark was an asshole who didn't love me the way I needed to be loved. We weren't meant to be. Better to not show for the wedding than put that ring on my finger and lie through the I-do's you know? Then I'd be in an unhappy marriage wishing I had never walked down that aisle in the first place."

"I suppose you have a point. Well, if you ever need to talk, you know…"

"I guess I know where to find you." I smile at him. "And thank you. I really do appreciate it."

"Alright then. So honest feelings about costumes from here on out?" He asks changing the subject back to the task at hand.

I give him a hardy nod. "Yes. Thank you. What's next?"

"Be right back."

He takes a little longer this time so I flip through my social media and take a quick close-up selfie so nobody can tell I'm wearing my wedding dress and post it to my profile letting my followers know we're preparing for tonight's festivities.

"Alright, coming out."

"I'm totally ready," I tell him, slipping my phone into the pocket of my dress.

Oliver steps out in his Mandalorian costume and with his helmet on there isn't a person on this planet who would know who he is.

"Wow! How do you feel in there?"

"Hot."

I nod. "Yeah. I wondered. I mean it might be nice for you because not a soul would recognize you and you could enjoy yourself without worry, but then again, having to wear that helmet all night could be a bit hot and or claustrophobic."

"Agreed. On to the next one."

I sit back in my chair, a contented smile on my face, and call to him in the dressing room. "Have I told you yet what an awesome guy you are for doing all this with me today?"

"You know, I'm not sure, so why don't you just tell me again?"

My smile widens at his request. "I think you're amazing, Oliver. And I'm super grateful you were willing to even consider doing this with me today. Ledger said I wouldn't be disappointed and so far, he was right."

"You have got to be kidding me," he mumbles from behind the dressing room door.

"No, I'm serious. Ledger is a very big Oliver Magallan fan. He had nothing but great things to say about you and if I'm being honest, I think you're—"

He swings his door open and raises a speculative brow at me. "Really?" he says with a smirk. "You thought this would be a good idea?"

"Holy fucking shit."

Yep. I totally said those words aloud just now.

As my jaw drops to my lap.

I can't stop staring.

Am I drooling?

I might be drooling.

I can't believe he even tried it on.

But there he is.

In the flesh.

Nothing but a loin cloth.

He is one fiiiiine ass—

"You know you're talking out loud, right?" Oliver pulls me from what I thought were my private thoughts. "I can hear every word you're saying and thank you for complimenting my ass."

"Wha-what?" I blink rapidly, trying to regain focus. "Sorry, your uh…your loin bulge has me a bit captivated."

"Another compliment." He chuckles. "I'll take it."

"Uh huh…"

"You know, my eyes are up here, Sweetheart," he finally says with a knowing glint in his eye.

Shit. Shit. Shit!

"I mean…" I shake my head, fanning my face because DAY-UM! "You would definitely turn some heads in that outfit, Oliver. I'm just saying. If you wanted to grab a woman tonight you would be—"

"I don't need to be grabbing anyone but you tonight, Scarlett. I'm your plus one, remember?"

I scoff out a laugh. "Honey, you can grab me all night long if you'll promise to wear that."

"Hmm." He smirks. "Almost worth it."

Are we flirting?

Is he flirting?

I think I'm flirting.

That's okay, right?

Ledger said Oliver's a great guy.

And he's single.

And I'm single.

I mean who wouldn't want to get with a man who looks like that?

I steal a glance upward and notice his face has grown serious and his brows are furrowed. "I'm not going to drop you at a huge party and leave you there, Scarlett. You know that, right? I'll be right next to you the whole time."

Why did I pick out this outfit?

Why did he have to look so unbelievably amazing in it?

Why can't I stop gawking?

God, to have just a piece of what he has to offer…

One-night stands happen all the time, right?

"Scarlett?"

"Huh? Umm, yeah. I mean, I'm just…you know. I'm just saying, if you met someone and wanted to…you know…"

"Not a chance," he says as his gaze locks onto mine. "I'm one hundred percent yours for the night."

He said it.

He's all mine.

For one night.

My body deflates against the chair and it takes every ounce of willpower in me to not lick my lips and call myself lucky.

For the love of everything holy, Oliver Magallan in nothing but a loin cloth is Hot. As. Fuck.

Tight abs. The perfect V that dips into his costume. Tattooed arms and a perfectly manscaped beard?

Yes please!

I clear my throat. "Alright. Umm, maybe we should try the last one then. I wouldn't want you to have to worry about, you know, falling out of that one or anything. Wardrobe malfunctions are a bitch, you know?"

"Right. Not to mention I wouldn't have anywhere to put my wallet and keys. This loin cloth doesn't have pockets." He winks and I snicker in response. He's such a good sport. I can't believe he even tried that thing on.

I mean, I'm grateful for the new core memory unlocked, but still.

"Well, for the record, if anybody were to ask or if you ever wondered, you would give Tarzan a run for his money."

Do not look at his bulge.

Do not look at his bulge.

Do NOT look at his bulge.

"Three compliments now? You flatter me."

Yeah, I'd like to do more than flatter you, big guy.

He winks at me again before stepping behind his dressing room door to try on his next costume. After a few quiet moments of me replaying images of Oliver in a loin cloth while he changes his outfit, I hear him murmur his approval.

"Whoa. This one is badass. I think this is it, Scarlett."

"Really? Let's see it!" I sit up, ready to see the perfect costume for my hockey player date.

He steps out of his dressing room and I can't stop smiling. "Oh, my God, Oliver! This is it! You look incredible!"

He stands before me in a dark blue V-neck drawstring shirt, his sculpted chest peeking through the lace-up front. God, he fills it out perfectly. His deep brown leather pants taper near the ankle and hug his strong legs. The leather belt with all the perfect Viking accessories hangs off his hips and the arm guards coupled with the fur collar… Oh, my God, it's perfect.

"You are…" I shake my head, speechless for a moment but smiling like a schoolgirl with a crush. "Oliver, you make one sexy ass Viking if I do say so myself. This costume is," I kiss the tips of my fingers, "chef's kiss perfection."

He turns a full three hundred and sixty degrees, allowing me the opportunity to take him all in. "So, this one's the winner?"

"Without a doubt. Yes. Rip those tags off, you sexy beast. The party starts in an hour."

"Alright. Let me grab my clothes and pay for this and we're out of here."

Chapter 5

Oliver

Since we have a little time before the party starts, we take some time to walk through a few of the other shops on the street, all of which are touting special Halloween activities and sales. Outside one of the small art galleries, there's a table set up for children to create their own Halloween themed paintings. Some are painting pumpkins and jack-o-lanterns, some have painted bats, and a few are creating their own haunted house complete with ghosts and magical sparkles and all sorts of colorful decorations.

"Wow! Those look amazing," Scarlett raves, a hint of excitement in her eyes. "You guys are pretty darn good at that."

The kids all smile and thank her for the compliments and one boy looks at me, his jaw dropped, his little eyes bulging. "Wait…are you?" His head cocks to the side as he takes in my costume and then he smiles. "Do you play hockey?"

I give him a mischievous shrug. "Maaaaaybe."

He gasps. "OH MY GOSH YOU'RE OLIVER MAGALLAN, AREN'T YOU?"

Scarlett beams as she watches my interaction with the kid.

"You're rather good, kid. What's your name?"

"Oliver."

My brows shoot up. "No way! Your name is Oliver too? How cool is that? You an Anaheim Stars fan?"

He nods enthusiastically. "Uh huh. You're my favorite player."

"Well shoot, that's so nice of you to say." I give him a high five. "It's not every day I meet a fan this far away from home. I wish I had something on me I could give you, but we're on our way to a Halloween party."

"How about a picture?" Scarlett suggests, gesturing to a woman standing behind him. "Is this your mom?"

The woman smiles. "Yep. I'm Mom." She shakes my hand. "It's very nice to meet you Mr. Magallan."

"The pleasure is mine. Yeah, we can totally take a picture. Let's do it, Oliver." Oliver's mom comes out from behind the table and I kneel beside him and smile for a few pictures. When we're done, he thanks me and wishes me luck in our next game.

"Thank you so much, Bud. I'm really glad I got to meet you."

Before we step away, Scarlett gathers the kids standing around and says, "Who wants to paint something really cool?"

Several small hands shoot into the air in hopes she chooses them and to their surprise, she picks every one of them. "Grab your paintbrushes and your favorite color because I think this dress needs a makeover." She smirks when all the kids gasp. Scarlett raises her arms and twirls in front of them. "Thirty seconds to paint wherever you want. Ready?"

"Yeah!" they all shout, dabbing their brushes into their paint.

"Okay, ready…set…GO!"

I step back and watch in wonder as the kids create splashes of color all over the white canvas that is Scarlett's dress. Pulling my phone from my pocket, I snap several pictures of her as the kids are painting. Her smile is sincere as she encourages each of the kids to make a colorful mess. She's truly mesmerizing as I watch her behind the lens of my phone camera. More than once today I've silently thanked the Gods, or at least Ledger, for encouraging me to do this with Scarlett because so far, she's everything I enjoy in a woman. Fun loving, adventurous, spontaneous, driven, and funny with a beauty about her that needs no filter. If she weren't going through the pain of recently being left at the altar, I could see myself asking her out.

But timing is everything and this is not the time.

Maybe someday.

———

Under the glow of the streetlights, we pass the famous St. Louis Cemetery No. 1.

Scarlett gasps. "Oh, my gosh, I've heard of this place! We have to walk through here."

I look at the sign posted near the gate and shake my head. "They closed almost four hours ago."

Her shoulders drop in disappointment, but then she cocks her head and walks along the gate several feet before turning back. "Let's go in anyway."

"What?" I nearly laugh. "Are you serious?"

"Yeah." She shrugs. "It's not like we'll be there to do anything bad. Just walk through. It's dark out. Nobody will see us."

"You know you're in a wedding dress, right?"

"Even better!" She beams. "If anyone does see us, they'll think I'm a ghost!" She grabs my hand. "Come on, please? Live a little with me, Oliver."

I consider her proposal and finally see the missing bars in the gate wall she noticed where we could slide in undetected.

What's the worst that can happen?

Ask forgiveness not permission.

If that doesn't work, throw money at someone.

"Alright, let's do it."

She claps her hands excitedly. "Eeek! Yes! This is the best. Come on. We've got this."

I follow her lead as she passes through the open spot in the gate. As she steps through, I hear a loud ripping sound and assume any moment now, her dress is going to fly off.

"What just happened?" I whisper.

She laughs. "My dress is caught on this broken piece on the gate. Can you help me?"

She points to where the bottom of her dress is indeed stuck on part of one of the bars that seems to be rusted away. I lift the ruffled material and can see the large rip in the dress.

"Scarlett, I'm sorry. It's really ripped up right here."

"Perfect! Give it a good yank. It'll be fine."

"Right. Trashing the dress. I forgot. So, you're good if I just pull?"

"Yep."

Giving the material a swift tug, it rips a little more but finally comes free and we slip through the rest of the way unscathed. Walking down the first row of graves, the place looks more like an old city. These are no tiny gravestones. Each one of them is a unique tomb or mausoleum, elaborate and crumbling from old age.

"This is the oldest cemetery in New Orleans," I tell Scarlett. "Did you know that?"

She shakes her head. "I didn't, but wow, I'm not surprised. This place is a wonderland for the unliving."

"Well, that's a different way of describing it."

She gestures to the buildings around us, some beautifully engraved, some with their own gates surrounding them. "I mean, look at this place. When my mom heard we were planning to come to New Orleans for our honeymoon, she told me about this famous voodoo witch that's buried here."

"Marie Laveau." I nod. "Your mom was right. She is buried here."

Scarlett's jaw drops as she glances at me. "How did you know that?"

"New Orleans is one of my favorite cities."

"But you don't play for their team? Why not?"

"When the agent says go where the money is, that's what you do when you're young. I could leave and try to get myself in over here now, but the Stars have grown on me. Now they're stuck with me."

She nods. "I understand that completely."

"You know who else has a tomb here?"

"Who?"

I smirk. "Nicholas Cage."

She halts, her brows pinching. "Wait…Nicholas Cage? But he's not dead yet. What the fuck?"

"He bought a tomb here anyway," I laugh with a shrug. "Some say he's hiding his fortune in the tomb. Some say he practices voodoo magic."

"Aaand what do you say?" she asks me.

"Meh. The guy just probably has a love for this place like I do and wants to be buried here. But who knows? I could be very wrong."

"You're just a treasure trove of trivia tonight, aren't you?"

"Say that five times fast," I dare her.

"Treasure trove of trivia. Treasure chove of chivia. Chesure chove of trivia. Chesheshure trove of chiv…yeah okay," she giggled. "I think I failed."

I wrap an arm around her shoulder. "Nice try through. Points for effort."

"But seriously. How do you know so much about this place?"

"What can I say? I'm a nerd when it comes to old spooky places."

"Ah, so you like the scary stuff, huh?"

"I've always loved Halloween," I tell her. "The parties, the horror movies, the silly decorations. It's just a fun, stress-free holiday for people of any age. I mean, who doesn't love Halloween?"

She catches my eye and studies me for several long seconds. Enough for me to cock my head and say, "What? What is it?"

Finally, she shakes her head and passes me a faint smile. "Nothing."

"You sure?"

"Mhmm."

Her change in demeanor catches me off guard. Something is clearly on her mind, and she doesn't want to share. Part of me wants to push it because I'm guessing she needs to feel like she can talk things out without judgement and she can with me. Maybe she needs this trip to heal from her ex leaving her at the altar and I honestly wouldn't mind being that person who holds her through it. But I'm not going to push it. Whatever is on her mind right now, I can only hope she'll talk when she's ready.

We walk endlessly through the darkened cemetery, pointing out interesting things about each tomb, laughing about our childhood and discussing our personal triumphs and tribulations. Not once does she ask me about hockey other than what I talk about and the overwhelming appreciation I feel for her because of that is indescribable. Anybody who meets me does nothing but talk about hockey. While some days I don't mind talking game, there are many more days I would much rather talk about anything else. Hockey is my job. Yeah, I love it, but it doesn't have to define all of me.

On our way back toward the opening we came through, there's a spot where the streetlights outside the cemetery seem nonexistent because of the larger sized tombs around us. Scarlett takes the opportunity to look up at the sky, the moon and stars shining brightly above us.

And then surprisingly, she lays herself down on the ground.

"Are you alright?"

"Mhmm." She pats the spot next to her. "Come join me."

"What are yo—"

"Come on, just do it." She raises her hand up, but I don't take it. Smiling at her goofy, spontaneous antics, I lower myself to the ground next to her, our shoulders almost touching.

My hand brushes up against hers as I lay next to her. "Now what?"

"Now we close our eyes and take a deep breath and just, I don't know, feel."

I turn my head in time to see her close her eyes beside me. She inhales and exhales deeply through her nose and then opens her eyes again to look up at the night sky.

"It's beautiful out here."

"It is," I confirm, though I'm not looking at the sky.

Because I can't stop looking at her.

"Do you ever just take a moment to drown out the world and everything around you and just marvel at the parts of our world that seem so…peaceful?"

"Like the ocean in the evening? Or first thing in the morning?"

"Yeah. Or the quietness of the mountains?"

"Sometimes I like to sit in the arena after practice once everyone has gone home. A huge vast room, and I'm the only person in it. It's a wonderful place to sit and think. A place where I feel comfortable and safe, where nobody can bother me because they don't know I'm there."

"Yeah," she whispers.

We lie in complete silence for a few minutes and then I hear the lightest sniffle. I turn my head just in time to see a tear slide down Scarlett's cheek.

Shit.

This is all hitting her.

Because as peaceful as silence can be, it can also open doors to all our demons.

Poetic, I know, as we're lying in a cemetery.

I could ask her if she's okay, but she's not talking, which tells me she doesn't want to talk about it. So, I do the only thing I can think of to let her know I'm here and she's not alone.

I shift my hand over a few inches until I find hers and entwine our fingers. She squeezes my hand like it's her lifeline and for the next five minutes I don't say a word while she cries in the quiet shadows in the city of the dead.

"Thank you, Oliver," she finally says softly, wiping her eyes and sitting up. "I'm so sorry."

"Hey." I slip a finger under her chin and turn her to face me. Her beautiful moss-colored eyes glistening under the light of the moon. "You don't need to be sorry for anything. He's an asshole for walking away from you, Scarlett. And he has no idea what he's lost."

Her weakened smile tugs at my heart. "Did Ledger pay you to say nice things to me, or are you actually this perfect guy who just happens to be his friend?"

I huff a quiet laugh. "I'm not perfect. Nobody is. We all have skeletons that bother us. But you're not alone. You're never alone."

"How is it that millions of people follow my life and pay attention to the things I'm passionate about, but just one man out of those millions can make me feel more alone than I've ever been?"

"Because he clearly never saw you the way I've seen you in just a few short hours."

"Yeah. You're right." She bows her head. "He never saw me. He never cared. And I knew it. I felt it back on day one when he had no interest in talking about my passions, but I ignored it. Denied my own feelings of inadequacy." Her shoulders fall. "Why the hell did I do that to myself? I knew he didn't love me for me. I knew it the whole goddamn time."

I inhale a big breath and release it silently. "You knew marrying the guy would make you comfortable," I answer her not knowing one thing about her fiancé other than the fact he is a douche who has a well-paying job. Her head lifts confirming my answer. "Stability and comfort aren't the worst reasons for marrying someone."

"But they're not the best by any means. I want to marry a man who loves me for who I am. Someone who listens to my pipe dreams and then encourages me to run after them. Someone who doesn't want me just for sex but for…love. But I don't want a husband who just loves me. I want my husband to be *in love* with me. Is that too much to ask?"

A few tears slip down her cheek and I wipe them away gently with the pad of my thumb. "You're a beautiful woman, Scarlett. Stunningly sexy even," I confess. "Any man will be lucky to have you by his side one day. And that man will love you for who you are and not force you to be someone you're not. So no, your idea of an ideal husband is not too much to ask at all. A husband should be in love with his wife. He should want to give her the goddamn world. He should want her every happiness and she his."

She wipes a few last tears from her eyes and then stares at me. "Yeah." She nods. "That's right. Thank you, Oliver."

The way she looks at me tugs at something inside my chest. Like a lost soul in search of its companion. Like she's hearing for the first time that someone else in this world gets her.

Understands her.

Cares for her.

Fuck, I wish I could kiss her right now and show her what it feels like to be cared for. She blinks a few times, her eyes lowering to my lips as mine do the same.

It would be so easy.

I could make this a moment for her.

For both of us.

But I don't want to take advantage of her when she's feeling vulnerable.

"Anytime. And listen if you don't want to go to this par—"

"Noooope. We're going." She shakes the sadness away and stands up much to my surprise. "I'm good. I promise."

"You sure?"

"Absolutely. I have you, don't I? My hot, sexy Viking?"

After tonight, I'm pretty certain you'll have more than I should admit.

I chuckle and take her hand. "I won't leave your side all night if that's what you want."

"Good. Let's get the fuck out of here. I need a drink."

Chapter 5

Scarlett

We head down to the warehouse district near the French quarter and pull up in front of Generations Hall. The building was an old sugar refinery at one time but has since been completely overhauled and redesigned into one of the most prominent event venues in the area. The Once Upon a Halloween Night party has been held here for the last several years. Oliver tosses his keys to the valet and opens the car door for me as I'm recording my entrance into tonight's party for my social media following.

"So excited to get inside and show you all this amazing party, but first, feast your beautiful eyes on my hunk of a date tonight, you guys!" I point my phone at Oliver. "He is none other than Mr. Oliver Magallan from the Anaheim Stars! And before you all ask, because I know you will, yes, he is, of course, a friend of my cousin Ledger who also plays on the team. And between you and me, he has seriously been the best guy to hang out with today!"

More than the best.

He really does seem like the perfect guy.

Perfect for me, anyway.

"Oh, my gosh, and look how freaking hot he is in this Viking costume!" I squeal and have him turn in a circle so my fans can see the full look. Oliver hams it up for my followers posing for them, flexing his muscles, and giving them the cheesiest of grins. "Is he not the best-looking Viking you guys have ever seen?" I pull my phone closer to my face and whisper, "And ladies, this one is single! I'll be sure to put in a good word for all of you, that is, if I don't snatch him up first." He chuckles and shakes his head as I send a wink to my fans. "I'll check back in with you all later! Ta-ta for now!"

"You do that with such ease," he tells me, offering his arm and walking me inside.

"Meh, it's easy to talk to nobody. You can't see them watching, and you don't have to care right away about what they think of you. And they know with me what they see is what they get. I don't use filters and I don't spend hours dressing myself to the nines to be a Barbie for them. I'd like to think that's what makes my followers appreciate me the way they do. I'm not fake. I'm not a diva. I'm just…you know, me."

"Well for what it's worth, I like…you."

I smile at him and squeeze his hand. "I like you too, Oliver. Let's get a drink so we can unwind and have some fun."

We walk together into Generations Hall, which is extravagantly decorated with all the spooky fun Halloween decorations you can imagine. Spiderwebs hang from just about everywhere, and green and orange party lights adorn the entryway. Several ghosts swing above our heads and a few skeletons have been set up and posed as butlers welcoming us in. Every single person here tonight is in costume. Even the wait staff are wearing black and white but their faces are intricately painted to look like half a skeleton face. It's impressive work for sure.

The darkened rooms create the right ambiance for a Halloween themed party, the black lights an extra fun touch. The effect on my dress makes me appear almost ghost-like as I float through the room to the nearest bar. The bartender is working on several drinks, setting them up in rows for the attendees tonight, each row with a different label.

Lucifer's demon drink.
Witch's Wish
Pumpkin Pie Shooters
Vampire's Cloak
Red Rum
Zombie Brain Hemorrhage

"Which would you like?" Oliver asks.

I narrow my eyes and twist my lips. "Umm, I think I'll start with a Vampire's Cloak please."

He grabs two of the Vampire's Cloak drinks, tipping the bartender with a fifty-dollar bill, and hands one to me.

"To a night of unfiltered fun," I toast, anxious to let this alcohol free me from my inhibitions.

"Cheers to that."

We clink our glasses together and I take a big sip, the sour taste of the tequila hitting my tongue.

"Time to dance!" I raise my glass and walk through the throngs of people already dancing, several of them recognizing me as I join in on the fun. We dance for what feels like hours, bodies grinding, hands roaming, and eventually Oliver is pulled away for a moment by a few fans who recognize him. I watch them chat and take a few pictures as I continue to dance, but when I spin back around I catch him watching me.

Like…*watching me*, watching me.

I move my body to the pulsing beat blaring through the speaker, my hips swaying as I give in to the rhythms and music. Holy Lord, the way his eyes are fixated on my body, the way his tongue glides effortlessly against his bottom lip, the feeling heats me from the inside out. In all the time I spent with Mark, he never once looked at me the way Oliver Magallan is looking at me now. Like I'm the prey he's hunting, like he wants me for his next meal. Damn, how does he make me feel desirable with just a glance?

I think if he asked me to, I would strip off all my clothes for him right in this very spot.

If he pressed me up against the wall and jammed his tongue down my throat I wouldn't stop him. Maybe I'm just horny, but damn, one look from Oliver Magallan and I want to be the one he spends his night pleasuring. I want to know what kind of lover he is. I want to experience everything he has to offer.

That is…if he's offering.

As his eyes roam up my body, they finally lock with mine and he doesn't look away. Like a magnetic pull, he steps closer to me without breaking my gaze, an unfamiliar flutter in my chest. His expression is ravenous as he approaches me. Seeing that he's no longer holding his drink, I shoot back the rest of my third glass and pass it, empty, to a waiter nearby and then I boldly grab Oliver's hand.

I place his strong hand on my waist and then turn so my back is against his chest. His hips respond when I start to move and I'm grateful he doesn't back away when my ass rubs against the bulge in his pants.

Holy hell.

What is it about parties and darkness and pulsing music that makes everything more sensual?

He grabs my other hip and holds me in place in front of him as we continue to grind together. I raise my arms as I dance and like a damn invitation, he slides his hands up the sides of my body until they're just underneath my breasts.

Jesus, yes.

I reach back and slide my hands through his hair, my body melding against his as we move together.

"Scarlett," he sighs in my ear.

Fuck, he has no idea how badly I wish he would cup my breasts in his hands. I turn in his arms and then clasp my hands behind his neck, his darkened eyes staring into mine. With a playful smirk I lift up on my toes to reach his ear.

"Live a little with me, Oliver," I purr. "I'm a poor jilted bride all alone on her honeymoon."

"Are you flirting with me, Scarlett?"

"I think I'm doing more than flirting, Oliver. I'm practically throwing myself at you. Because I like you. Please don't let me fall."

A hint of mischief crosses his face. "I just needed to hear you say it."

"You're looking at me like you want to kiss me."

"I wanted to kiss you in the cemetery."

"Is that so?"

"Mhmm."

"What are you waiting for then?"

He nips at my earlobe. "Permission."

"Granted."

He slides his hand to my ass, pulling me against him as tightly as he can, his leg shifting between my thighs. With his other hand on the back of my head, he pulls my face to his and crashes his lips against mine. I smooth my hands up the sides of his torso and then glide them down his chest. He groans against my mouth and though I can't hear him above the sound of the music blaring through the speakers, I can feel it. When I dip my tongue between his lips his control begins to unravel. Resting his forehead against mine, he blows out a steadying breath.

"Fuck, Scarlett. What are you doing to me?"

An unwelcomed pang of guilt shoots through my chest. "I'm sorry Oliver. If this isn't what you—"

"No, no, no." He shakes his head, cupping my face in his hands. "I'm not saying I don't like it. You're…" His gaze lowers to my lips and then moves back to my eyes. "You're beautiful, Scarlett. And that kiss was, well, obviously you can feel the effect it had on me," he explains, referring to his stiffening cock between us.

"I just don't want you to think I'm trying to take advantage of you. That's all."

"Like I'm a woman in distress, you mean? Because my fiancé left me at the altar?"

He bobs his head. "Well…yeah. I mean, don't get me wrong. The moment I saw you at the airport I knew you were someone special. Someone I wanted to know. And I like you. Maybe I even like you more than I should because we barely know each other but—"

"No buts, Oliver." I lay my finger against his lips, halting his words. "We're both adults and if I didn't want to kiss you, I wouldn't have. I like you too," I tell him with a smile. "You're fun and adventurous and you haven't poo-pooed any of my crazy ideas yet."

"I don't think they're crazy at all. Spontaneity is good. Life is too structured to have a plan all the time. It's nice to let go and live a little."

I raise up on my tiptoes to reach him better and lift my chin until our mouths connect. He slides a hand through my hair, slightly pulling it to angle my head the way he wants to deepen our kiss, and then sweeps his tongue between my lips. He is without a doubt a passionate kisser and I find myself wishing I were dressed as a naughty nurse or a French maid with a short dress on instead of this gown that doesn't provide the easiest access.

Because holy shit, there is a pulse between my legs that is dying for some attention.

I break our kiss and then smile at the man who seems to only have eyes for me.

"Then let's spend this time together living and let whatever happens, happen."

"I like that idea."

Chapter 6

Oliver

Taking a reprieve from the main dance floor, we stroll through the rest of the building noting some of the amazing costumes others have chosen for tonight. We've seen everything from zombie ballerinas to murderous nuns to eighties punk rock skeletons to angels with sparkling tutus. Every costume is unique, and some extremely impressive in the amount of detail and work put into them.

We make our way into one of the rooms serving appetizers to grab a quick bite, bumping shoulders with several others as we wait our turn. Standing in line, Scarlett and I say hello to a couple dressed as movie stars from the seventies, as well as a man dressed as Robin Hood and his date in a unique butterfly masquerade costume. As Scarlett laughs with them all, I snap a few pictures of her on my phone. She's in her element, being the social butterfly. I chuckle to myself because she should be wearing the butterfly costume her new friend is wearing. How apropos.

What I fail to notice while taking pictures is one of the skeleton crew staff members carrying a bowl of marinara sauce to the table to accompany the mozzarella sticks. In her chat with her new friends, Scarlett flings her arms out, hitting the crew member and causing him to spill the marinara sauce all over her dress.

Though half of his face is covered in face paint, his expression is nonetheless horrifically remorseful. The side of his face not covered in makeup turns ashen and his body stiffens.

"I am sooo sorry, Ma'am," he says with a tremor to his voice. He brings a hand to his forehead. "Oh, my God. I can't believe I just did—"

"Stop right there." Scarlett lifts a finger, her jaw clenched tight as she stares at the man. With marinara sauce now dripping down the front of her dress, she turns her head around as far as she can to try and see the back of her dress. Finally, she spins so the back of her dress is facing the frightened staff member and angles her head back beaming at him. "Can you do the back as well?"

The couples around us look on, a bit shocked, but I throw my head back in laughter.

That's my girl.

The crew member shakes his head, confounded. "Ma'am I...I don't unders—"

"Oh, my apologies. Allow me to explain," she tells everyone around us because yep, she's that girl. "My fiancé left me at the altar last week."

Looks of sympathy and concern all around.

"And I know, I should probably be crying in my bedroom surrounded by cartons of ice cream and alcohol, but I'm not, because if I'm being honest with myself, he didn't love me the way I deserve to be loved. He never supported the life I wanted to have for myself. It was always about his career. His money. His life. So, it's all good. I'm here celebrating the honeymoon we should've had and it's on his dime because he already paid for it."

Our new friends laugh with her, some even giving her a high five.

"So, I'm trashing this dress! The perfect dress that at one point meant so much to me. The dress I was supposed to wear when I became a wife. The dress I'll take off at the end of the night and burn because who would want to keep this memory? So go on," she tells the crew members. "Please, you're going to get a new bowl of sauce anyway. Drip the rest of that on the back for me."

"You're sure?" he asks.

"Absofuckinlutely."

We all stand by watching the crew member artfully drip the rest of his sauce down the back of Scarlett's dress before he scurries back to the kitchen for another bowl.

The girl in the butterfly masquerade costume nods her approval. "For what it's worth, I think what you're doing is amazing."

"Thank you very much."

"I'm Polly, by the way." She offers her hand. "I would hug you but…" She gestures to the sauce and Scarlett laughs, returning her handshake.

"No problem. Totally understand. Scarlett Dayne."

"I've seen you a few times in my Insta feed. I really love your energy. Your always such a bright and positive person."

"Doesn't do us any good to spread hate, right?" Scarlett answers. "Anything but love and kindness is exhausting if you ask me."

Polly nods. "So right."

As we move up in the line, and grab a plate for our food, Scarlett asks Polly, "Hey have you tried these pot stickers? Are they good?"

"Oh my, gosh, yes! This is our second time through. They're pork-filled and you must try them in this Szechwan sauce. It's to die for!"

"Sold!" Scarlett laughs. "Thank you for the recommendation. It was lovely to meet you."

"Pleasure to meet you. Hope you guys have fun tonight." Polly and Robin Hood take their filled plates and head outside. After grabbing a few appetizers, we find a spot where we can eat and watch the rest of the action going on at the party. The DJ announces a costume contest and several people have lined up to participate.

I gesture to the group. "Who do you think will win."

Scarlett studies the group of participants. "Hmm, my money is on either Medusa, or that guy dressed as Edward Scissorhands."

"Mmm." I nod. "I would have to agree. But that mime is definitely a crowd pleaser."

"For sure."

When we finish our light snack, I take Scarlett's plate and throw away our trash and then take her hand back in mine. Quite frankly any reason to be touching her, to have my hands on her, is perfectly okay with me. "Where to next?"

She looks around and spots a sign at the bottom of the stairs with an arrow pointing to the second floor for VIPs to receive a special palm reading. Her eyes light up. "Ooh let's do it! Our passes are VIP! You in?"

"You believe in that kind of stuff?" I ask, having never been into the whole cosmic-fortune-telling-zodiac kind of thing.

"I don't not believe in it, I guess," Scarlett answers. "I want to believe ghosts are real even though I've never actually seen one, so, you know…" She shrugs. "Yeah, I guess I can believe in it. I'm at least curious to know what she has to say."

How bad can it be?

"Then let's do it."

We climb the stairs to the second floor and follow one of the signs to a small nook area where an older woman sits at a small round table. She's dressed in a ragged long purple dress with tiny silver and gold sparkly beads sewn in starry patterns. There are a few mixed metal and leather necklaces around her neck as well as a few metal bangle bracelets around each wrist. Her headband even matches her dress and the feathers hanging from her hair are a nice touch.

"Hello, my dears," she greets us. "I had a feeling I would be speaking with you this evening."

Sure lady. You clearly say that to everyone.

She motions for us to take the two seats opposite her, and once we're seated and comfortable, she smiles at us, a few teeth missing but no worse for the wear.

"You would like a palm reading tonight, yes?"

Scarlett nods. "Yes, please. I've never had one done before."

"Well, my name is Rowena and I will be your oracle for this evening. Now, which is your dominant hand?"

Scarlett gives Rowena her right hand and watches in awe as Rowena turns it over, examining and feeling her skin and then studying the lines on her palm for several quiet moments. She gives Scarlett's hand a gentle squeeze and then presses along the sides.

"Ah, this hand has bounce to it," she states. "This means you have a natural refinement about you and an energy loved by many." She presses down on Scarlett's fingers and tugs her thumb back slightly, nodding with each movement. "You show flexibility in your aura and you are very generous. Your pinky finger stands out from the rest of your hand. This means you are of strong business mind; you communicate well and are quite independent."

"Now, let's get to this beautiful palm." Rowena brings a magnifying glass to Scarlett's hand, tracing some of the lines in her palm. "Ah, yes, doors are opening for you, my dear. Prosperity and success look good for you." She smiles and wipes her hand down Scarlett's palm like she's trying to soothe it, her brows furrowed. "I am sorry for the heartache you have endured for it was surely not your fault…"

Scarlett flashes me a confused glance but it's not like her life hasn't made headlines. Rowena could've known she was coming. She could've read about Scarlett's failed wedding in any of the Hollywood media outlets.

"But rest assured, young one, people you care about will grow closer to you and you will live a long and very happy life. You will even gain a sister."

"That's impossible," Scarlett whispers. "I'm an only child."

Rowena pats Scarlett's hand. "This line here tells me you are a late bloomer," she says. "And while that might be sad news as a young girl, as an adult, you should know that the best is yet to come."

Scarlett's brows peak. "Well, that's good to know."

"You are a hopeless romantic and looking forward to your happily ever after."

Internally I roll my eyes.

That's too easy to say to a woman who is literally wearing a bridal gown right now.

"And I am happy to tell you, you will find love, but you will find it far from home. You tend to step into the water of your life with one foot out and one foot in, but my dear, I will tell you that you will gain all the things in life you most desire if you jump into that water with both feet."

Finally, she lets go of Scarlett's hand and sits back in her chair.

"Thank you, so much," Scarlett says with a smile. I can already tell she's trying to put all the pieces together to make sense for her.

Rowena nods and then lays her hand open toward me. "You next?"

"Uh, sure."

I give her my left hand to study and she does so with much curiosity. She turns it over, her fingers smoothing over the lines of my palm, and then she shakes her head. "This is not your dominant hand, my son."

Wow.

How did she know that?

"You're right," I tell her with a mischievous smile. "I was trying to trick you."

Rowena laughs. "Happens all the time, but Rowena sees all and knows all."

I switch hands and she takes a few moments to touch my hand, squeezing the sides and flexing my fingers this way and that.

"This is a strong hand. The energy of this hand is heavy but protective." She traces a few lines on my palm. "These lines here, by your thumb. They are the bands of duty and responsibility. Yours are deeply etched." She chuckles quietly. "You are strong and mindful but can be stubborn at times."

Scarlett giggles next to me, the sound of her happiness putting me at ease. I like her laugh. I like her smile. I like it when she's happy.

Really I just like everything about her.

"You have a managerial spirit that tells me you thrive in a position of responsibility…"

I'm not the Captain of the Stars for nothing.

"But emotionally you are sensitive. You don't like to hide your feelings."

Fuck, how much of me can she really see?

"You are not an overindulgent man. You prefer quality over quantity."

Scarlett snickers next to me. "That's what she said."

Rowena pats my hand. "You have worked very hard to find yourself and you are confident in your strengths, but your personal life has taken a back seat to all other aspects of your life."

You could say that again.

She looks me in the eye, holding my gaze for an uncomfortable moment before she smiles and nods as if we just spoke telepathically.

We didn't. I swear.

"I see great things for you, my son." She leans forward in her seat. "But heed what I say, for many who have come before you have chosen the path of disbelief and have therefore denied themselves their greatest joys." Squeezing my hand, she covers it with her own and says to me, "Your love will not always be your passion. Your passion is not always your love. A family man you will be, with a supportive and rewarding partner by your side who will be your greatest cheerleader."

When?

When is that supposed to happen?

She pats the top of my hand and then sits back in her chair smiling at the both of us. "It was a great pleasure meeting you both."

I pull out a few twenty-dollar bills and leave the tip for her in the marked jar on her table.

"A pleasure meeting you as well," Scarlett says with a slight bow. "And thank you very much for your time." I give a curt nod to the woman and then take Scarlett's hand leading us back downstairs.

Scarlett squeezes my hand. "Well, what did you think?"

"I think she said a lot of interesting things."

"Your love will not always be your passion. Your passion not always your love," she recalls what Rowena told me. "What do you suppose that means?"

"If I'm relating her words to my own life, I'm guessing she means hockey won't always be my passion. Or that my passion for hockey won't always be the most important thing in my life."

Can't believe I'm actually saying that out loud.

I live and breathe hockey right now.

Can't imagine ever giving that up.

Though I suppose the day will come when my body gives it up for me.

And God knows I really would love a family of my own.

"That's kind of deep," she says. "You okay with hockey not being your life? I imagine it's pretty damn important right now."

"Of course. It pays the bills. It's what I do. It's who I am. But sometimes it's not bad to be reminded that one day hockey won't be my life anymore and what will I have then, you know? There are more important things in life than hitting a puck around the ice for points."

Scarlett gasps playfully. "You better not let anybody hear you say that mister hockey star."

"You're right." I drag my hand through my hair. "Think you can keep my secret?"

Scarlett rounds on me, wrapping her arms around my waist. "I think if you kiss me, the secret moves from you to me. Then I become the secret keeper."

"Ah. So that's how it works?"

She nods. "Mhmm."

"Perfect." I lower my mouth to hers, releasing my secrets and passing them to the one person who I wholeheartedly believe would hold them and protect them for me for as long as I needed. Her soft tongue slides across my lips and dips inside my mouth and fuck if my body doesn't want to react in every way possible.

On any given day I eat and sleep and breathe hockey.

But today, everything about the game of hockey is out the window.

Because I just want to eat, sleep, and breathe Scarlett Dayne.

Chapter 7

Scarlett

"How do you make it so easy to breathe, Scarlett?" Oliver asks me, his forehead pressed to mine.

"Because I don't expect you to be someone you're not, Oliver. You're free with me. Zero expectations. Consider me your safe space."

"I'm finding myself overwhelmingly attracted to you," he says. "And I'm sorry if that's too much. Maybe Rowena was right. I'm not good at hiding my feelings."

"It's perfectly fine to have feelings. I have them too." I bring my hands to his cheeks. "I wasn't sure how this day was going to go, but somehow, you've managed to make every moment perfect. You let me take the lead instead of treating me like your personal arm candy. You've asked about my feelings. My desires. What I want for myself and for my future. Do you know how long it's been since a man has asked how I feel? Hell, I could marry you right now and have no remorse given what I was about to walk into."

"I'm really fucking glad you didn't marry him."

"Me too."

His lips move with mine in a soft, slow kiss, breathing against me as we share in what is turning out to be a beautifully intimate moment. One that makes my toes curl and the insides of my body tingle. The more I allow myself to let go and feel all of my feelings, the more I know I have to tell him what's been on my mind since we walked into this party.

"Oliver?"

"Yeah."

"I want you."

God, I've never been so bold in my life.

Please don't turn me down.

It will crush me.

"Stay with me tonight."

He cups my face and gazes into my eyes, a deep and prolonged stare, like he's diving inside my soul. "Are you sure that's what you want?"

I slide my hands down his chest, my fingertips brushing against his warm skin through the V cut of his shirt. "I'm dying for you to touch me and as much as I would love to take the risk right here right now," I tell him as my heartbeat pounds through my body. "It wouldn't be good for either of us if we were caught being indecent in public, so yes. Please. Stay with me."

My cheeks flush as my entire body heats at the mere mention of what we could be together.

His gaze falls to my lips as his hand cups the side of my face. "You're so goddamn beautiful. I give him a heated smile before he tilts my mouth up and lowers his down over me. He's gentle for only a moment and then his grasp on me changes. His hand moves to my hip where he grips me, pulling me tightly against him. The intensity of his hold on me mixed with the heady lust I feel for him has me feeling things I've never felt in my life.

Not with Mark.

Not with anyone.

Oliver's tongue slides smoothly into my mouth taking whatever he wants and I give it to him freely. His lips work mine and before I know it this kiss has become one of those unforgettable moments where the rest of the world disappears because the only two people that exist right now are me and Oliver.

"You want to get out of here?" He finally murmurs against my ear.

"Mhmm."

"Good. Let's go." He takes my hand and leads me outside to the valet. We wait only a few moments while the valet pulls our car to the curb. Oliver escorts me to the car, his hand on the small of my back and then he opens the passenger side door for me, helping me with my gown as I climb inside. He tips the valet, generously I'm sure, and poses for a quick selfie before hopping inside. I give him the address to the hotel, which ironically ends up being the same place Oliver is already staying, and then we're off.

Tapping my hotel key card against the keypad on the door, I push it open and step inside, Oliver right behind me. I flick on the lights and take in the spacious room. A king-sized canopy bed is the obvious focal point, trimmed in black and lavishly decorated in ivory and rich golden hues.

"Wow, this is stunning."

I step to the window overlooking a tree-lined St. Charles Street, marveling at the beautiful mansions one after another.

"Stunning is the perfect word." I hear Oliver behind me before I feel him. He wraps one arm around my waist, his front to my back. With his other hand, he scoops my hair out of the way and kisses my neck once, twice, three times. "You are indeed stunning, Scarlett Dayne."

As he runs his tongue along the shape of my neck up to my ear, he slips his hand underneath the V-neck halter of my dress and palms my breast. I inhale a sharp breath at the pleasure of his touch and my head falls back to his shoulder.

"Oliver…"

"I've been wanting to touch you like this all night. It's your honeymoon, Scarlett," he murmurs in my ear, sneaking his other hand into my dress and over my other breast.

God, his touch feels amazing.

Strong hands.

Warm.

Protective.

Adventurous.

"What kind of man would I be if I didn't give you all the attention you deserve while in your honeymoon suite?"

I try to keep my breathing even but that is sooo easier said than done with Oliver Magallan holding my breasts like his two favorite prized possessions and pinching my nipples between his thumb and forefinger. "It would probably make you an asshole."

"Right," he chuckles. "And I'm no asshole, so I'm going to need to do something about this."

A tingling pleasure floods my body with every swoop of his fingers against my nipple, my lips separate enough for me to tell him, "I think you're off to a fine start. Do you think you could help me out of this dress?"

"It would be my greatest pleasure."

He unhooks the halter piece around my neck and then slowly undoes each button down my back, his lips caressing my skin with each button's release. When he gets to the last few buttons, the dress falls around my feet, leaving me in nothing but my black satin panties. He trails his hands up my legs to my thighs and then feathers them up my sides and across my shoulder blades.

"Gorgeous." He kisses the base of my neck. "I'm going to need you to turn around so I can look at you."

I do as he asks and he takes me in slowly, shaking his head. "Fucking beautiful, Scarlett."

I give him a confident smirk and a teasing shrug of my shoulder. "Well, now that you have me here, what are you going to do with me?"

He tears off his Viking accessory belt and with a hand behind his head he grasps the neckline of his tunic and pulls it off.

Yesssss!

Finally, I get to see him like this again.

He pulls me against him and lifts my chin with his finger. "I'm going to lay you out on that gorgeous bed over there and eat my weight in pussy gold until you come on my tongue."

Fuuuuuck. Meeeeeee.

"And then with your permission, I'm going to bury myself inside you and we're going to fuck like two people who are made for each other."

He kisses me, tugging my bottom lip between his teeth and then licking away the pain.

"Like two souls that have been searching for their mates for years…" He kisses me again, this time trailing his fingertips down my sides. "But tragically only get to be together for one night."

His tongue pushes past my lips this time. "One very…hot…sweaty…mind blowing night."

"Oliver…" I pant. His words and the feel of his body against mine create a pool of pleasure between my legs, sparking a flame inside me. "Yes…please!"

He lifts me into his arms and carries me to the bed where he lays me down and grabs a couple pillows to position under my hips. Leaning over me he circles his tongue around one of my nipples, sucking it into his mouth, hard and rough at first, and then soft and smooth to soothe away any pain, the perfect combination of spicy and sweet.

"Fuck, Oliver." My back arches off the bed. "Give me more. I like it rough."

"Not a chance, Sweetheart," he replies, moving to my other nipple and repeating the same movements. "If I only get one night with you, I'm taking my slow, sweet time. I'm savoring every inch of you." He kisses my chest between my breasts and then moves south, running his tongue along my abdomen, down to my pelvis overtop my panties.

"I want to breathe in every scent," he says before he dips his head between my legs and inhales a deep breath.

"Oh, my God," I whisper as he hooks his fingers into the crotch of my panties and pulls them down, letting them fall to the floor. He pushes one foot out to the side and lifts my other leg, hooking it over his shoulder. Settling himself at the apex of my thighs, he parts me with his fingers and then lazily drags his tongue through me.

"Oh, fuuuck, Oliver."

For the love of tiny baby Jesus Christ.

This man's tongue has magical powers.

Where did he learn this voodoo magic?

He circles his tongue up and around my clit, spreading my arousal all over me and moaning with satisfaction.

"Shit, Scarlett. You're fucking intoxicating."

"Oli…"

"I swear to God, I could get drunk on you and you alone."

He goes in a little more ravenous this time, his beard rubbing against my ass as he licks me repeatedly, rounding my clit and flicking it with his tongue.

I'm surely going to die right now.

I'm going to die a most glorious death, crying out for Jesus as I combust from the most wonderous orgasm I've ever had.

"Oliver, I swear to all the Halloween voodoo gods if you stop right now, I'll never forgive you."

He chuckles against my skin, the vibrations of his voice intensifying the pleasure he's already giving me. He slides two fingers inside me, pulling them up against my inner wall, caressing that hot spot while blowing and sucking on my clit.

"Oh, my GOD, Oliverrrrr! Do NOT stop!"

I writhe against his face as he takes my clit between his lips, sucking and flicking so hard and fast he takes my breath away. Surprising me, he reaches up and caresses my breast, rolling my nipple between his fingers, and I'm a goner. My hand in his hair holding him against me, I scream his name as I come on his fingers and against his lips.

"That's it, Sweetheart." He drags his fingers from inside me and sensually sucks them into his mouth. "The best meal I've had in days."

"Oliver, that was…" I try to breathe but hell. His tongue took the wind right out of me.

"That was…" I bring a hand to my chest reminding myself to take a deep breath and release, deep breath, and release, and then I give him the most satiated smile I can muster.

"That was incredible."

"Please tell me you come like that for every man you're with because if you only come that hard for me, it will be so fucking difficult to have to walk away from you when our time is up."

A tiny piece of me breaks apart inside at the thought of this wonderful man walking out of my life forever. I know to some it might seem like a one-night-stand or quick rebound recovery from my stupid ex, but there is something about him that has me wishing for more time. More laughs. More adventures. More kisses. More touches. Shaking my head, I answer him honestly.

"Oliver no man has ever made me come that hard."

"What?" His brows pinch. "You're serious?"

I swallow the lump in my throat and nod.

"Fucking hell, Scarlett." He wipes his hand down his beautiful face.

"Can I tell you something else?"

"Of course."

"I've never wanted to feel a man inside me, filling me, taking me, as much as I want to feel you. Please tell me you suck at it, because when you walk out that door, I don't want to have to spend the rest of my days dry and barren because I experienced the best fuck I will ever have and nobody else will ever compare."

He reaches into his back pocket and pulls a condom from his wallet and then he removes his pants and boxer briefs, his perfect and impressive cock at the ready. His eyes solely on me, he rips open the condom packet and sheathes himself. Hovering over me, his weight on his forearms, he kisses my forehead and then my cheeks and my lips.

"Sweetheart, no matter what, when I'm done with you, nobody else will ever compare."

I whimper below him. "That's what I figured, but it's a risk I'll just have to take."

"That's my girl," he says to me as he lines himself up, dips his cock into my arousal and thrusts inside me.

"Moooother fuck," he hisses.

My eyes roll back in ecstasy, and my jaw drops as I inhale at his exhale. "Are you okay?"

"Fuck yes," he answers. "Scarlett, you're…Christ, you're so fucking tight."

I slide my hands up his chest and kiss his shoulder. "And wet just for you, Oliver."

His eyes squeeze closed as he pulls mostly out of me but the moment he pushes back in, his gaze is on me. "It's too much," he says, shaking his head. "Jesus, you feel amazing.

I reach up and kiss his lips, holding his face in my hands. "Then take me, Oliver. Fuck me as hard and fast as you want, but wherever you go, take me with you."

He doesn't give me any other warning before he pulls out of me and slams back in so hard my head nearly hits the headboard. He thrusts into me over and over, so unexpectedly hard I wonder for a fleeting moment if he might tear me apart.

"Scarlett…fuck. It's too good. It's so fucking good."

Reaching down between our bodies, I circle my finger around my clit, heightening my pleasure as he pounds into me. He shakes his head in disbelief at the visual.

"Beautiful."

"Oliverrrrr, I'm close."

"Me too, Sweetheart." He leans down to kiss me, and I moan all of my feelings into his mouth, spurring him on.

"Fuck, Scar. Fuck, I'm going to come. Come with me."

"Yes! Oliver, yes. Touch me. Please!" I beg. He answers my request and reaches out, grabbing my breasts. Squeezing them, brushing his thumbs against my nipples and pinching, not once slowing down his thrusts. "Oooh, my God!"

I inhale several sharp breaths and then moan in one massive climactic release.

"Shit. Fuck, Scarlett, your pussy is clenching around me. Shit. I'm…" His muscles tense and he begins to shake above me. As his body stiffens and he releases inside me, he cocoons my upper body in his arms, holding me against him. His moan one of the most satisfying sounds I've ever had the pleasure of hearing.

"You, Scarlett Dayne, are an amazingly wonderful woman."

"And amazingly sweaty," I tell him with a smile. I'm not exactly sure where to go from here. Is he planning to stay? To go? If this is also his hotel, what's the harm in sleeping here tonight with me? To try and prolong his stay as much as possible, I ask him what he's thinking.

He grins. "I'm game for round two in the shower if you are."

I climb over him until I'm straddling his lap. "I thought you'd never ask."

He spanks my ass lightly and then lifts me easily from the bed, carrying me into the shower. "Let's get wet and make a lot of noise."

Chapter 8

Oliver

I have to go.

I may miss my flight as it is.

But she's just so fucking beautiful. Awake and smiling or asleep and comfortable like she is now, she's breathtakingly gorgeous and I don't want to have to stop looking at her. Once she fell asleep last night, I stayed awake as long as humanly possible so I could run my fingers through her hair and watch her breathe against me. Sleep against me.

It felt wonderful.

But our time has come to an end and I have to get to Chicago.

Not wanting to be the cause of broken hearts or mixed feelings, I quietly slide out of bed and into my regular clothes. I don't even brush my teeth. I'll do it at the airport. I don't want to wake her. Before I grab my bags and head out, I grab a pen and the small notebook from the hotel room desk and scribble a note for her so she doesn't feel like I carelessly walked out on her.

I would never do that.

I couldn't do that.

But waking her to say goodbye might crush me and I'm already grieving the loss of what she feels like in my arms as it is.

Leaving my note on my pillow for her, I take one last look at my beautiful bride and then quietly open the door and slip out. Once in the car I think back on all the fun we had together yesterday and the passionate lust-filled night we had last night.

Leaving Scarlett this morning to fly to Chicago is one of the hardest things I've had to do in a long time. I knew if I didn't leave before she woke up, I would never want to say goodbye. Having her fall asleep in my arms after the best four rounds of sex I have ever experienced in my life was a fucking dream. Her softness, her warmth, the way she smiled at me after every orgasm, like she's always known I would show up in her life and show her how she deserves to be loved, made me feel like I had a purpose. And for the first time since I can remember, she had me wondering what life outside of hockey could look like.

What life with her could look like.

Hopefully, she'll forgive me for my chicken scratch of a note I left for her. She has my phone number so she does have the ability to text me, though I haven't heard anything from her yet today. I should be glad for that, I suppose, but then what if I hurt her by not saying goodbye? What if she woke up and saw she was alone and went right back to feeling like she did on her wedding day?

Fuck.

Nothing was supposed to happen between us. We were two adults spending a fun evening together. That was the deal.

So why do I feel this overwhelming sense of loss?

"What's the matter with you?" my sister asks me from the other end of the couch.

"What? What do you mean what's wrong with me?"

"You're not your regular self."

"In what way?"

"I don't know." She shrugs. "You just seem…down."

Milo pipes in from the kitchen. "Probably because he knows we're going to kick their asses tomorrow night."

"Keep talking, Landric." I smirk and send a reassuring wink to Charlee who shakes her head at the banter her husband and I have had all day. Trying to change the subject, I gesture to her growing baby bump.

"So how are you feeling? We haven't talked much about your pregnancy."

She nearly gets teary eyed talking about it. "I'm feeling great most days and I'll admit, it's nice to work from home. Milo just lets me bum around in his sweatpants and of course my favorite sweatshirt, so I'm always comfortable."

I pretend to gag at the sight of the extremely purple Wile E. Coyote sweatshirt Charlee is wearing. Milo has owned that thing for way too long, except honestly, it looks cute on my pregnant sister. And for just a split second, an immense feeling jealousy washes over me.

She found the love of her life in the most unexpected way and now she's about to start a family. I met Scarlett in the most unexpected way, yet here I am alone and missing her.

"What about you?" she asks after we laugh over Milo's ridiculous taste in clothing.

"What about me?"

She shrugs. "I don't know. Tell me something new about you. Is there a special someone in your life? You don't talk about your dating life much?"

"Uh, pot calling kettle, Sis. I seem to recall you living with this asshat for several months before you ever told me what was going on in your life."

She blushes, her hand smoothing down her stomach. "Okay, okay. I've apologized for that about a billion times. I'm just asking because I want to see you happy. That's all."

I nod, taking a deep breath and realizing maybe I just need to get it out in the open.

"There's a girl."

Charlee sits up, a fresh excitement in her eyes. "Yes! I knew it! Tell me everything."

"There isn't a ton I can tell you, honestly."

"Where did you meet her?"

"New Orleans." I cringe when I give her my answer.

Charlee's brows rise. "Oh. Sooo, you mean you just met her? Or is she like, you know, someone you meet up with whenever you're in town."

"She's not a booty call, Charlee."

She raises her hands in defense. "Just asking."

"I did just meet her yesterday. Spent the entire day and all night with her and I know this sounds crazy as fuck but…"

"You like her."

I nod slowly, my eyes finally meeting Charlee's. "Yeah. I really liked her."

"Liked?" She frowns. "Why liked? You can't work out a long-distance thing?"

"With my schedule? That would be insane. But ironically…or maybe not, I don't know, she's actually from L.A."

"Wait, what?" Charlee moves to the edge of her seat. "Oli, that's not that far from Anaheim! What the fuck?"

"I know but—"

"No buts. Is she married?"

I almost laugh. "No."

"Kids?"

"Nope."

"Then what's the problem?" Milo asks, coming around the coffee table and plopping down next to his wife.

"Hell, I don't know." I drag my hand through my hair. "No, that's a lie. I do know. It's not that she's married because she's not. But she was just left at the altar a couple of weeks ago. Like, when I met her yesterday, she was literally wearing her wedding dress."

Charlee eyes me curiously. "Uh, why?"

"Oh, we went to the big Once Upon a Halloween Night party together last night and she wanted to go as a jilted bride and trash her dress."

"Oooh, I've always wanted to do that."

Milo turns to Charlee. "Excuse me?"

"Sorry," she laughs. "I mean I always thought it was a cool idea and if I had had a dress from Jared—thank God we never married—I would've wanted to do something like that." She wraps a loving hand around Milo's arm. "Don't worry babe. You're stuck with me."

"So yeah, anyway, we've known each other for twenty-four hours. I certainly wasn't going to profess my love for her and ask her to commit to a relationship when she hasn't had enough time to grieve the relationship she just got out of."

Charlee cocks her head. "Did she tell you she was still grieving this other relationship?"

"No. But she did cry a little while we were laying in the cemetery."

"What?" She shakes her head, confusion etched on her face. "Why were you—"

"Don't ask. Long story. And it was a beautiful moment."

"Okay well, what I'm trying to say is, you don't get to choose how long she needs between relationships. That's for her to decide. For all you know you're the perfect one for her because this other guy clearly wasn't and if that's the case, why wait another minute? You're not children being forced to wait, you know. When it's right, it's right."

"Okay, well, it's a little late now. She's there and I'm here."

"Dude, if you want her enough, you'll figure out a way," Milo says, wrapping an arm around my sister. Of all the hockey players I know who could've been a great partner for my sister, I really am glad she found Milo Landric. He's a great guy with a solid head on his shoulders. There's never a doubt that he's head over heels in love with her, and that's what Charlee deserves. Especially after the hell she's been through. "It's never too late. Make it special. Do something unique for her that shows you how much you like her."

Charlee narrows her eyes and turns to her husband. "Is that what you did for me?"

"Uh, yeah. Of course."

She folds her arms over her pregnant stomach. "Like what?"

"I read to you, Goldilocks. And we uh, you know, we did yoga."

He winks at her, and she cracks up laughing. "Alright, I guess I can give you that."

"Also, I beat the hell out of your asshole ex on the ice. Best game I ever played."

"Even after winning the Cup?" she asks him.

He kisses her sweetly. "Absofuckinlutely. The fucker got what he deserved."

Conversations Scarlett and I had yesterday start spinning through my head. Of her hopes and dreams and all the things that drew me to her.

Can I really do this?

Can I pull it off?

Will she go for it?

It would be amazing to see her again.

To take her on a proper date.

To spend time together in our own homes and familiar places.

Hmm…what if…

"So, you don't think it's creepy for two people to possibly fall in love in one day?"

Milo shrugs. "Fuck a day. Falling in love only takes a moment."

Charlee turns and looks at Milo with a loving smile. "My moment was the night you carried me to your room and read to me."

Milo nods. "My moment was the day I opened my penthouse door and saw you on the other side of it."

Charlee's shoulders fall and she starts to cry. "Milo! You can't say things like that to a hormonal pregnant woman!"

"Sorry babe," he says pulling her against him. "But I speak the truth."

Smiling at them both, I lay a hand on Charlee's knee. "Hey thanks for the advice, guys. I think you may have sparked an idea."

"That's what we're here for man," Milo says. "Let us know if we can be of any help. The guys and I are getting pretty good at grand gestures when it comes to the ladies."

Chapter 9

Scarlett

My body hasn't felt this sufficiently sore, in all the best ways ever, in my history of sex. Mark was not by any means a fierce lover. He was a missionary all the time kind of guy and if he got off before me, so be it. It sucks that it's taken being left at the altar to realize what I had with my ex was not what I thought it was in my heart. That all this time I was simply convincing myself that a life with Mark Adleman was the kind of life I wanted.

Now I beg to differ.

Now I know that kind of life isn't what I want at all.

I deserve better.

I deserve to wake up every morning with the man of my dreams.

I deserve to have my body worshipped like it was last night.

I deserve to be able to wake up so sore that I need a warm bubble bath to rejuvenate my tight muscles from all the intense but oh, so enjoyable sex the night before.

I deserve to be happy.

But when I roll over in this big comfy bed expecting to feast my eyes on the divinely sexy and sleeping Oliver Magallan, I find his side of the bed empty. No sign of him or his luggage. Nothing except for a note lying on his pillow. Opening the folded paper ripped from the notepad on the desk, I read his words.

Good morning, Gorgeous.

I know if I had woken you to say goodbye, I would've missed my flight and possibly my next game and well, with fame comes responsibility, right? In all honesty though, I find it extremely hard to resist you and felt it would better for both of us if I just left peacefully rather than drag any of our emotions into my departure. But I can't leave without saying one thing.

You are an amazing human being, Scarlett Dayne.

Okay, maybe two things, because I'm not done. The way you aim to live your life, spreading love and kindness, your proclivity for spontaneity, your energy in making messes, and your inner peace are what make you a beautiful person. I sincerely hope you can follow your heart in all that you do when you head back home. That you continue to be brave and take chances. Remind yourself the brave don't live forever, but the overly cautious and those who dampen your light don't live at all, Scarlett.

Our time together is something I will NEVER forget. Thank you for encouraging me to let go and "live" with you. It meant more to me than you know. Until we meet again…and I hope we do meet again…

All my love,

Oliver.

His note clutched to my chest, I lie back on my pillow and stare up at the bed canopy. "Dammit. He's really gone."

It's not like I didn't expect this.

I knew at some point we would have to say goodbye to one another. I guess the selfish part of me wanted to experience waking up next to a man who genuinely cared for me. A man who put my feelings first. A man who found me sincerely attractive. Even if for just a fleeting moment.

Tears spring to my eyes as I read his note a second, third, and fourth time.

"I miss you already, Oliver."

He was right to leave when he did. Knowing me, I would've bawled my eyes out and begged him to try and figure out a way to make a relationship work. Or I would've pretended what we had was no big deal, played it off until he left, and then drowned my sorrows in a bathtub with a bottle of tequila.

When I posted on social media that I was looking for a plus-one for last night's party, never in a million years did I expect to fall for the guy who would end up being my date.

But here I am.

Alone, again.

And missing his presence more than I ever thought possible.

—

"Hey Scar! How was the party? How was the date? What shenanigans did you get into today? Are you out there finding your inner peace?"

Sniffles greet my best friend on the other end of the line. "Hey Maria."

She gasps. "Oh noooo! What's going on? Who do I need to kill? Should I bring a shovel?" She lowers her voice to a mere whisper. "Seriously, are you alright?"

"I'm alright," I answer. "Just feeling down is all."

"Aww, I understand, Babe. This is good. You've needed to get all your feelings out and maybe New Orleans was right where you needed to be to release them."

"Maria?"

"Yeah Babe?"

"What if…" *Do I really want to ask her this?*

Yes.

"What if New Orleans was right where I needed to be to fall in love with my actual soulmate?"

Silence falls between us, followed by an emphatic, "I'm sorry, WHAT?"

"Do you believe in love at first sight? Or I don't know…love at first…meet?"

"I mean, I want to believe it's possible, so sure. Why are you asking? Did you meet someone at the party?"

"No. I met him when I got off the plane. He was my date."

She really gasps this time and then chuckles. "You're falling for Oliver Magallan?"

"I don't know," I cry. "I mean, maybe? Is it possible? Can two people fall in love in one day? Because ever since he left, I've done nothing but think about him all day and the absolutely amazing time we had together last night and Maria, I think I really like him."

"Okay…"

"But seriously, who falls in love with a guy they just met in one day?"

She laughs. "Uh, just about every fairytale princess known to man with a few exceptions."

"Touche."

"You asked."

"You're right, I did."

"So, alright, you like the guy. Did he seem to share the same feelings?"

"I think so…but Maria what if I'm so off on this one? What if I put myself out there again only to have him break my heart? I can't believe I'm saying this, but I fear if that were to happen, it could hurt worse than Mark."

"Ouch," she replies. "For Mark I mean."

I huff out a laugh. "Yeah well, the truth hurts sometimes."

"It does. And you just answered your own question. The truth can hurt sometimes, but you'll never actually know the truth if you don't put yourself out there and try. I mean honestly, Scarlett, he's not that far from L.A. You could potentially make it work."

A twinge of hope sparks in my chest.

Is it really possible?

"Do you think?"

"Uh, relationships have been built with a lot further distance between them before, so yes. Absolutely. You just need to convince yourself to jump in with both feet instead of keeping one dry just in case."

Jumping in with both feet.

Oh, my God.

That's what Rowena said too.

What if…

Could we…

I won't know if I don't try.

Live, Scarlett.

Swiping any residual tears from my eyes, I sit up on my bed and notice my trashed wedding dress in a heap on the floor. My plan was always to trash it and burn it, but now the more I look at it, another idea floats through my head.

"Alright, Maria. I think I'm going to go for it."

"That's my girl! Whatever you do, you've got this, Babe. You can do hard things! Trust me, you would much rather regret the chances you were brave enough to take than regret the ones you never took because you were too scared to take them."

"Exactly. I've got to go. I have a plan to make."

Maria gasps, startling me. "Holy shiiiiit."

"What? What's wrong? Did something happen?"

"Uh, Scarlett?"

"Yeah?"

"Have you been on social today?"

"Not since this morning, why? Oh God. Was Mark having an affair this whole time? Am I now the laughingstock of social media? What kind of damage control am I going to have to do?"

"Negative on all that, babe. It's good news. I won't bother telling you, but when you hang up, I would check in if I were you."

"Uh, okay."

"Love you babe. Good luck with your plan. Call me if you need anything."

"Thank you, Maria. I'll update you later!"

I press the button to end my call and immediately open my social media accounts. To my shock and surprise, my name is trending.

"What the…"

As I scroll through posts, I come across Oliver's account and click to open his profile. My face heats and my heart melts at the numerous pictures he's posted of me from last night, memories of us I never knew he was catching, along with the couple of selfies we took together.

The caption in his post reads:

To my newest crush. I think Rowena was right. About everything. Do you believe?

"Holy shit!" I scream a little louder than appropriate in a hotel room but I don't care.

I scroll through each of the pictures and read the hundreds of posts from fans of mine and of Oliver's wishing us the absolute best and hoping his post means what they think it means.

God, I hope he means it too.

As I'm reading through more comments, a message comes up in my direct messages so I click on it.

Charlee Landric: Hi Scarlett. Allow me to introduce myself.

My name is Charlee. Charlee Magallan Landric. I am Oliver's

younger sister. I know, I know, if he knew I was writing to you right now, he would never forgive me for butting into his relationships, but holy shit once I saw his social media post, how could I not? *smiley emoji* Giiiirl, he's crazy about you!! *heart emoji* He spent the night with Milo and I last night and was telling us all about you and how he didn't want to leave you and he felt terrible about it. And he was all sad and boo-hoo because this man is in luuurve! And maybe this is just me being the super romantic type because I edit romance books for a living or maybe it's that I'm very pregnant which means very hormonal but I need to know your feelings on all of this because if there's a chance his feelings are reciprocated, then I have to get you here to surprise him! I may be married to a Chicago Red Tails player, but oh, my God, if my brother goes on the ice like the depressed sad sap he was today, beating their asses at tomorrow's game will be all too easy and I don't want him to have to deal with that blowback on his performance because you know, he's my brother and I love him. Soooo....girl talk?

Me: OH MY GOSH! I can't believe you just wrote me and fuck YES!!! GIRL TALK!!!

Charlee Landric: Perfect! Send me your number and I'll call you!

Chapter 10

Oliver

"No way is Joe the best one," August argues. "Everyone knows it's Kevin."

"But Joe was married to Sophie Turner, Harrison states. "The girl from *Game of Thrones* and she's hot as fuck."

"Ah didn't know you were a sucker for red-heads, Harrison." I laugh. "Besides, Kevin is married to a nice girl who isn't in the media all the time. They probably have a nice quiet life together. It's the perfect situation."

"Bullshit." Griffin huffs wrapping his stick while still in his rubber duckie pajama pants. Seriously, he's the only man I know who can pull off wearing the world's wackiest pajama pants any time of day. "Kevin's a softie. Nick Jonas is the sexiest of them all and he has the best voice hands down." He finishes the wrap on his stick and leans it up against his locker, then stands with his hands on his hips. "Any other debates we need to have before we kick ass tonight?"

Ledger tosses out, "Back Street Boys or NSYNC, Griff?"

Griff huffs. "Uh, I'll take Justin Timberlake on his own for one thousand, Alex."

"Aaaaand who's your favorite Golden Girl, again?" I ask, knowing exactly what he'll say.

He places his hand over his heart. "Listen, my girl Rose will always have my heart. She's so fucking sweet and her life in St. Olaf was clearly filled with educational adventures, but Dorothy was given all the best sarcastic comments. I've got to give props to her."

Everyone has a soft spot for Rose.

"Hey, Magallan, I forgot to ask," Ledger says, lifting his chin my direction. "How'd it go with Scarlett? Did you guys hit it off?"

Oh yeah. We hit it off, and we got off.

"Uh, yeah, actually. We had a fun time." I busy myself with my skate laces so they can't see the blush on my face.

"Did you get laid?" Griffin teases.

Ledger smacks his arm. "Hey, that's my cousin you're talking about."

Griffin shrugs with a smirk. "You don't hear him sayin' no, do you?"

Fuck.

A silence falls over the room and I glance up from my skates to see what's going on.

They're all staring at me.

Double fuck.

"What are you all staring at me for?"

Ledger's eyes grow in his blank stare and I can't tell if he's mildly excited or mega pissed. "Did you fuck her, Magallan?"

"I…" Letting go of my laces, I lower myself to the bench. "I'm not going to lie to you, man. Yeah. We…"

"HOLY SHIT, DUDE!" Ledger barrels over to me, nearly crushing me in a bear hug. "Are we going to be related now? I knew you two would hit it off! I just had this feeling. It's like I was psychic or something. Tell me everything." He cringes. "Oh, but don't tell me about the, you know, the fucking part. We're family and all so I don't want to know about that."

Griffin sits next to me, batting his eyes like a dufus. "Uh, we do, bro. Sharing is caring."

"Fuck off, man." I push Griff away with an eye roll and a smile and then I take a deep breath and let the guys in on my thoughts.

"Look, my time in New Orleans was amazing. Scarlett was…" I shake my head. "A breath of fresh air. We didn't talk hockey once and I found myself thinking more and more about the idea that one day hockey won't be my life anymore and that if I don't start living something other than my life on the ice all the time, I won't have anyone to share the rest of my years with. She showed me that. It's like being with her showed me what it's like to just live in the moment. No plans. And it was…incredible."

Ledger prods. "So, you guys are going to be a thing, right?"

I shake my head. "That's not how I left it."

"What? What do you mean?" His disappointment matches how I felt leaving her.

"I wrote her a note and then left before dawn because I didn't want to hurt either of us by prolonging the inevitable."

"So, you didn't even make plans to see her again?"

I shake my head. "No. I mean, she has my number and she could text or call at any time. I sort of left the ball in her court. And she hasn't tried to contact me since I left so…"

My shoulders fall. "I don't know. Maybe I really upset her by leaving without saying goodbye. Maybe I fucked it all up. I've felt like a shmuck since I left."

Ledger shakes his head. "I wouldn't count yourself out yet, man. I say wait till we get back home and have a day off and then call her. We're not that far from L.A. Seeing her wouldn't be impossible."

"Yeah." I shrug. "Maybe. Unless I break down and end up writing her tonight after we win and I'm high enough to do something potentially damaging to my ego."

Harrison chuckles from his seat on the bench. "So, you like her then?"

"Yeah," I answer unequivocally. "I do. I know this might sound really stupid but I think I might even more than like her. I'm drawn to her. I haven't stopped thinking about her."

Ledger pats my back and passes me a reassuring smile. "This is all good news, bro. We're going to help you get the girl when we get home. Whatever you need. Whatever we can do."

"Thanks guys. I think for now, we focus on kicking a little ass tonight. They're not going to just hand this win over to us."

We're all suited up and ready when Bear comes through the door. His uniform and pads are on, but his game face looks anything but normal as he shakes his head, confused.

"You alright there, Bear?"

"Yeah." He hitches his thumb behind him toward the door. "Just passed this girl in the hallway with one of the Red Tails staffers."

Griffin pipes in. "Was she hot?"

He shrugs. "She wasn't not hot. Harrison might like her. She had dark red hair and she's wearing this wedding dress that looks like she pulled it straight from the trash."

I swear, my body stands on its own accord. "Did you say wedding dress?"

"Yeah. Paint and stains and who the fuck knows all over it. What do you suppose—"

I don't wait for Bear to finish before I run for the door, pulling it open and bolting through staffers in the hallway as fast as I can on my skates.

"Scarlett?" I shout down the hallway as onlookers give me curious glances.

"Scarlett Dayne!" I check the pressroom window but she's not in there, so I continue on through the next set of double doors and that's when I spot her.

"Scarlett!"

"Oliver!" Her smile is like the goddamn sunshine on the cloudiest of mother fucking days as she runs toward me, crashing into me and wrapping her arms around my neck. "I believe, Oliver. I one hundred gazillion times believe!"

Her reference to my social media posts earlier brings a smile to my face and a huge sigh of relief to everything else. I squeeze her body against my pads as hard as I can. Anything to be able to feel her again.

"I'm so fucking happy to see you. I can't believe you're here. What are you—"

My words are cut short when I spot my sister standing with the woman I believe to be Colby Nelson's wife a few steps away. "Charlee."

"Yes," Scarlett answers. "Don't be mad at her Oliver. She saw your post and wrote to me and I'm so glad she did. The moment I woke up in an empty bed I missed you. I knew then that I wanted you. I just wasn't sure of your feelings."

"My feelings?" I laugh.

She leans back so she can see my face. "Yeah, your feelings."

"Well, let me see if I can make myself a little clearer." Lowering her so her feet hit the floor, I turn around and back her up against the wall, cupping my hand behind her head and kissing her gently with as much passion as I can muster when my heart is literally pounding itself right out of my chest.

"I want Rowena to be right, Scarlett. I want you to be the cheerleader by my side. I want you to be my greatest love. More so than any game of hockey. I know it's fucking fast, and I'm more than willing to slow down if that's what you want or what you need, but Scarlett Dayne, I want you in my life. No, I need you in my life. And I want to be in yours. Every adventure. Every crazy idea. I want to give you everything you could ever want."

She lays her palm against my heated cheek. "All I want is you, Oliver."

"Thank fuck for that," I murmur before I lean in and kiss her again. When we come up for air, I take her hand. "You're staying for the game, right?"

"Of course! Charlee and I had dinner earlier and she said I could sit with her and the Red Tails wives."

I stop and look at what she's wearing, my eyes narrowed. "Well, you can't sit with the Red Tails crowd like that." I pivot and shout down the hallway. "Hey Stephens!"

Our uniform manager turns my direction as I pull off my jersey, the cool air hitting my chest. "Get me another jersey, will you?"

He smiles and shakes his head. "Sure thing, Magallan."

I tug my jersey over Scarlett's head. It's huge hanging on her body, but that's okay with me. The more of me on her, the better as far as I'm concerned. "So, are we burning this dress tonight when we get off the plane?"

She shakes her head. "Not a chance."

"What? Why?"

"Because this is my lucky dress, Oliver. Without it, I wouldn't have you." She tugs at the colorfully stained ruffles. "Look at it. It's filled with memories of us. Our first lunch together, our painting adventures with those kids, lying in the cemetery together, drink stains, marinara sauce…all the fun we had. It's all right here in this dress, so I don't ever want to get rid of it."

"I love it." I kiss her again. "Make me a promise."

"Anything."

"Promise me, when we get married one day—and we will get married one day—you'll wear this dress."

She laughs. "Oh, my God I would love to. Will you make me a promise too?"

"Anything you want."

"Promise me you won't ghost me at the altar. My heart could take it the first time, but with you? It would crush me."

"I'm not him, Scarlett. You're it for me. You're the only one I want. I want to be wherever you are."

She rests her forehead against mine, kissing my lips lightly one more time.

"I love hearing you say that."

"I just have one more question for you, and then I have to get back to the team so we can get on the ice for warm-up."

"Okay."

"How do you feel about the Jonas brothers?"

The end

Want more of the Anaheim Stars team? Read on for an excerpt of August Blackstone's upcoming story in *WHAT IF I TOLD YOU* releasing October 23rd!

WHAT IF I TOLD YOU
Chapter 1
August

"You going to shove that whole wiener in your mouth at one time?"

Griffin eyes the hotdog in his hand and then winks at me. "Nah. Just the tip this time." I watch in amusement as he licks the end of his hotdog bun and then bites off the end chewing as his eyes roll back in his head. "Fuck, so meaty." He turns the end of his hot dog around so I can see where he took a bite. "And just look at that girth."

Harrison leans forward in his stadium seat and pulls his sunglasses down his nose. "Dude, do you need a minute alone with that thing? In a private room perhaps?"

"Hell no." Griffin smirks. "I like eating wieners out in the open. Right here in front of all of you." His brows shoot up as an idea floats into his mind. "In fact, I think you all need a good wiener experience. Where's that wiener man? WEINER MAN? I NEED YOUR BIG WEINERS!" He shouts as the crowd around us chuckles. I've never been more grateful to be wearing sunglasses but then this is Griffin's everyday behavior so am I surprised?

Not in the slightest.

"Someone shut him up," Barrett mumbles from a few seats down before he tips back his beer and swallows what's left in his glass. "The last thing we need is the media writing headlines about the team's wiener obsession."

"You think I could deep throat this one, Bear?" Griffin asks dangling the rest of his hotdog in front of his face with this mouth wide open. "Ten bucks says I could do two at one time."

"No bet,'" Barrett responds. I have to laugh as Oliver Magallan and I glance at each other. Even in the off season Barrett "The Bear" Cunningham is in a grumpy mood.

"Dude, Bear, you alright down there big man?" I ask him. "You need someone to deep throat your wiener?"

"You offering Blackstone?"

I rub my chin playfully and pretend I'm giving the idea some thought. "I tell you what, if the zombie apocalypse ever comes, I'll make sure you're well serviced right before we turn, alright? Instead of death coming for you, you will be coming hard for death."

"Fuck the zombie apocalypse. It's never going to happen." He shakes his head and wipes a few sweat beads from his forehead. Nothing like a ninety-five-degree July day to take in a baseball game with the guys. We're used to the ice and the cold temperatures so while this is a nice change, it's also hot as fuck.

"You know what you should worry about though?" Ledger Dayne adds to our conversation from behind us.

I turn my head slightly so he knows I'm paying attention. "What's that?"

"You should worry about the twat apocalypse, because that shit's already upon us, bro."

Playing along, I grab my phone and swipe my weather app open. "A twat storm you say? Are we about to have an overwhelming number of twats at our disposal? You call that an apocalypse, but I call that a normal Saturday night."

"Riiiiight." Griffin Laughs beside me. "Like you've seen in influx of anything of the sort lately."

"What?" I shrug. "How do you know whether I have or haven't?"

"Uh, how about because you tell me about every piece of tail you capture. I'm like your virtual bed-post marker. The keeper of your fucks if you will and so I'll just come out and say for you, dear friend, it's been a minute."

My smile fades because damn, he's right. It has been a minute.

"Aww, it's okay August. We all go through dry spells once in a while."

"Hey look who's up to bat," Oliver motions to home plate. "That's Carter Matthews, he's the brother of one of Charlee's friends. And I think now brother-in-law to Zeke Miller."

Oliver's sister, Charlene AKA Charlee, lives in Chicago. She's married to Milo Landric who plays for the Chicago Red Tails, so now because of Oliver we've hung out a little with the whole team. Great bunch of guys. I wish we got to spend more time with players from other teams sometimes. Once or twice a year on the ice is never enough and we don't get to be us when we're on the ice anyway.

Carter swings at the first pitch.

"Strike one." Griffin says before he leans over to me and asks, "So why the dry spell?"

Carter swings again with the second pitch and misses for a 0-2 count.

"I don't know." I shrug my shoulder. "I think I'm bored."

"Bored?" He laughs again. "How the hell are you bored? It's summertime. How are you not out tapping every woman you come in contact with? How are you not traveling to all the remote islands of the world?"

"Alone?" I scoff. "I'm not taking some stranger on vacation and I'm definitely not going alone."

"I don't know." Griffin Shrugs. "It worked for Magallan."

Carter swings at the third pitch and makes contact with the ball. We watch as it flies to the outfield and Carter runs all the way to second base.

"What about me?" Oliver asks.

Oliver Magallan. Our team captain fell in love with a girl after accompanying her on her honeymoon over Halloween last year. Ledger's cousin, Scarlett, was ghosted at the altar. Poor thing. Apparently, she was a bit of a mess, but she took it in stride and put out an all-call on social media for a date to the year's biggest Halloween party that was supposed to be part of her honeymoon. Ledger thought it would be a good idea for Oliver to go with her so he kind of set up their agreement and the rest is history. Who knew he would fall for some girl on her honeymoon?

Me though…yeah, I haven't been that lucky. Not yet anyway.

"Oh I'm just reminding August here that you were lucky enough to fall in love with Scarlett after taking her on her honeymoon."

"Yeah well, we'll call those extenuating circumstances," I Say. "Ledger's related to Scarlett and he knew Oliver would be good for her."

Griffin huffs a laugh. "Oh, so that's what you want?"

"What?" I ask tossing back my beer.

"You want me to set you up with someone?"

I nearly snort at Griffin's suggestion coughing on the beer that just went up my nose. "No fucking thank you. I can find someone to eat my wiener perfectly fine on my own.

"A warm body, yeah. But we're not talking about pussy."

"Then what are we talking about?"

"You said you were bored," he reminds me. "Maybe you need a woman. Like an honest to God relationship."

"And why would I do that? I'm not home for several months out of the year. Our schedule is rigorous and I have women throwing themselves at me everywhere we play. No girlfriend or wife wants to see that. It wouldn't be fair to her."

"Then how do you think Oliver and Scarlett make it work?"

"Easy," Oliver jumps in. "Scarlett is a social media guru. She travels just as much as we do and quite frankly, she could basically follow the team wherever we go doing whatever she wants to do and her followers would follow us so really, it's a win-win for them, for her, and the team."

"Alright wise-ass." Griffin turns back rolling his eyes. "You might be right about that, but what I'm trying to say is I bet you two aren't bored. You have each other. You have someone to wake up to every morning and go to bed with every night. You laugh, you talk, you enjoy each other's company. Life is better when you have someone to share it with and maybe that's what August needs."

"Says the single guy who hasn't had a serious girlfriend in at least three years and has been playing with his wiener in the middle of this baseball game."

"Ooh." He scowls. "Ouch. You wound me."

"Just telling it like it is. I'm not the only one in a dry spell."

"He's not wrong there." Ledger adds.

"Alright but I like to see my friends happy so leave it to me to play matchmaker. Ledger's in love with Marlee Remington so I've got to work on that one."

Ledger's eyes bulge and even in the summer sun I can see his face turn red. "What? I am not. Why would you say that?"

"Because it's true dude. We all see the way you look at her."

He slouches in his seat. "Yeah well she never looks at me."

"She will Ledge." Griffin pats Ledger's knee. "I promise, one day, she will." He turns back to me. "Now, what about that girl?"

I roll my eyes and take another sip of my beer watching the next batter for the Indianapolis Racers connect with the ball for a homerun.

Dang. Anaheim is not having a great game.

"What girl?"

"You know," he adds, wiping his face with the hem of his tshirt. "Your friend. That one you facetime every week."

My brows peak and I nearly spit out my drink when I realize who he's talking about. "Ella?"

"Yeah. Her. How about her?"

Now I do laugh. "Dude, she lives on the entire other side of the country first of all. Secondly, she's nowhere near my type and thirdly, if she would've heard you just now suggesting that the two of us hook up she would be laughing even harder than me. And she'd probably give you the finger."

"Oh." Griffin frowns. "I guess I just assumed you two were in love or you had this secret relationship you didn't want to tell anyone about."

Harrison raises his hand but continues to stare out at the field. "Not going to lie, August. I thought that too."

"Same," Oliver adds.

"Yep." Barrett says with a belch.

I shake my head emphatically. "No way, guys. Ella's just a friend. My very best friend. I've told you that. We've known each other for…pfft…basically since we could walk. If we were going to be an item, that would've happened a long fucking time ago. Besides, if we were having a secret relationship, you certainly wouldn't ever see me fucking other women in a goddamn hotel after a game. Not that you see that, you know, literally. I'm just saying. I would be loyal as fuck to her. She's too good of a person to deserve to be cheated on. I'd fuck up the asshole that ever did that to her."

Griffin gives me a little side eye and then shakes his head. "So, you two never…?"

I snicker with a shake of my head as well. "Not a chance. Well," I stop short. "We did kiss once."

"See? I knew it!" Griffin's eyes bulge as he points at me. The rest of the guys laugh quietly.

I lift my hands in front of me. "Whoa, slow down. It wasn't like that, I promise. We were like twelve. Maybe thirteen but not quite in high school yet."

Griffin twists his mouth. "Oh."

"Yeah. We agreed to kiss each other, you know, be each other's first, so we could both learn what it felt like and it was terrible. And by that I mean we were both terrible at it. First it was this tiny peck on the lip and then we didn't know what to do with our tongues so let's just say it was a gross wet mess that tasted like Swedish fish and sour cream and onion Pringles."

"Oh, my God." Ledger snorts. "Okay, that's funny shit."

"Yeah we both laughed about it after the fact and promised never to tell anyone and certainly never to try it again. So don't tell her I told you anything."

Griffin crosses his heart with his fingers. "Cross my heart."

I don't miss Ledger and Oliver crossing their fingers and giving each other a high five. I roll my eyes frustrated with myself for breaking my own rule. Never tell the guys anything you don't want coming back to bite you. That little tid-bit I just dropped is definitely going to bite me in the ass one day.

"Anyway, we watched each other date lots of…" I shake my head. "Wrong people over the years. We've always had, and still have to this day, one of those relationships where I can tell her anything, you know? And I know she doesn't judge me for it because she knows me and I know her. And I've always reciprocated that for her. She tells me all sorts of random shit whether I need to know it or not."

"What does she do?" Harrison asks.

Griffin tilts his head. "Isn't she like, a professional cheerleader or something?"

"No. She's a cheerleading coach back where we went to college."

"And how would you feel if she lived out here?" Barrett asks from the end of the row. Seriously, I didn't think he was paying much attention to this conversation.

Elated.

Happy as fuck.

Like my life is complete.

Like I have someone to really share life with.

"Why do you ask?"

"Because I heard Marlee Remington talking to one of the other ladies in the front office about how Stockler is moving."

All of us turn our heads toward Barrett, our jaws dropped in shock.

"Kingston Stockler? As in our team mascot?"

He nods. "Yeah. I guess his wife got a promotion at work which means they're moving to Seattle. He's going with her to help with the kids. He's always said his family comes first."

"You think Ella should apply to be the team's mascot?" I ask him but he merely shrugs.

"I'm not saying yes and I'm not saying no because I don't know who the fuck Ella is except that appears to be some imaginary friend you supposedly talk to every Tuesday night. But if you're as close as you say you are, you might want her to be out here and her background sounds like she might have the right experience. I guess you would have to talk to front office."

My thoughts start to run with the idea of Ella applying to be the team's mascot.

Would she want that?

Could she do it?

Of course she could do it.

She would be great at it.

And she'd probably love every minute of it.

"So, they're replacing Kingston?"

"I imagine they will, yeah." Barrett nods.

Oliver places his hand on my shoulder. "DO you think your girl would want to give it a go?"

"She's not my girl, and really…" I turn back in my seat. "I seriously doubt it. That would mean a huge move for her. Not sure that's really something she wants. She seems really happy where she is."

WHAT IF I TOLD YOU is available now at Amazon!

OTHER BOOKS BY SUSAN RENEE

All books are available in Kindle Unlimited

The Anaheim Stars Hockey Series
What If We Do – Jilted Bride Novella
What If I Told You – Childhood Best Friends
What If I Knew You (coming January 2025)

The Red Tails Hockey Series
Off Your Game - Angry Meet Cute
Unfair Game - Strangers/Roommates to lovers
Beyond the Game - One Night Stand/Surprise Pregnancy
Forbidden Game -Teammate/Best Friend's Sister
Saving the Game - Fake Relatonship
Bonus Game - Single Dad/Nanny

The Bardstown Series
(*Prequel*) I LOVED YOU THEN: Second Chance at love
I LIKE ME BETTER: Enemies to Lovers/workplace
YOU ARE THE REASON: Second Chance
BEAUTIFUL CRAZY: Friends to Lovers
TAKE YOU HOME: Boss's Daughter

The Camel Club Series
Smooch: One Night Stand/Strangers to Lovers
Smooches: Single Mom/Ex's Best Friend
Smooched: Fake Relationship/Surprise Pregnancy

The Schmidt Load Novella Series
You Don't Know Jack Schmidt
Schmidt Happens
My Schmidt Smells Like Roses

Stand Alone Novels
Hole Punched: Strangers to Lovers/Hidden identity

Total Ship Show
(part of Love at Sea multi-author series)

Kamana Wanalaya for the Holidays
(She-grinch/sunshine trope)

No Egrets : Grumpy Sunshine
(Part of the Tuft Swallow Multi Author Series)

The Village series

I'm Fine (The Village Duet #1)
Save Me (The Village Duet #2)
*The Village Duet comes with a content warning.
Please be sure to check out this book's Amazon page before
downloading.

Solving Us
Surprising Us (a Solving Us novella)

KEEP IN TOUCH WITH ME!

Website: authorsusanrenee.com
Liinks.co/authorsusanrenee

Facebook.com/authorsusanrenee
@authorsusanrenee
Instagram: @authorsusanrenee
Twitter: @indiesusanrenee
Tiktok: @authorsusanrenee

About the Author

International bestselling author, Susan Renee, wants to live in a world where paint doesn't smell, book boyfriends are real, and everything is covered in glitter. An indie romance author, Susan has written about everything from tacos to tow-trucks, loves writing romantic comedies but also enjoys creating an emotional angsty story from time to time. She lives in Ohio with her husband, kids, three dogs and a cat. Susan holds a Bachelor and Masters Degree in Music Education and a self-awarded Doctorate in Sass and Sarcasm. She enjoys laughing at memes, speaking in GIFs and spending an entire day jumping down the TikTok rabbit hole. When she's not writing or playing the role of Mom, her favorite activity is doing the Care Bear stare with her closest friends.